D1216326

LOST RIVER CANYON

When old Sam Bovard confronted Marshal Evan Stannard, a stranger suddenly appeared and Bovard lay dying — killed, some said, by his estranged son James. Then a bushwhacker shot at the marshal and injured James' own son, and the hunt for him was on. That was where Lee Bovard, James' niece, came in. Stannard never dreamed he would ever be following a woman tracker, but he was going to be very grateful that she was also a deadly shot.

Books by Ray Kelly
in the Linford Western Library:

SHENANDOAH

C.1

RAY KELLY

LOST RIVER CANYON

Complete and Unabridged

LINFORD
Leicester

First published in Great Britain in 1997 by
Robert Hale Limited
London

First Linford Edition
published 1998
by arrangement with
Robert Hale Limited
London

British Library CIP Data

Kelly, Ray
Lost river canyon.—Large print ed.—
Linford western library
1. Western stories
2. Large type books
I. Title
823.9′14 [F]

ISBN 0–7089–5328–X

Published by
F. A. Thorpe (Publishing) Ltd.
Anstey, Leicestershire
Set by Words & Graphics Ltd.
Anstey, Leicestershire
Printed and bound in Great Britain by
T. J. International Ltd., Padstow, Cornwall

This book is printed on acid-free paper

1

A Man Killer

It was the kind of country which the Indians had fallen back into during the closing years of their wars against the whites. It was rugged, timbered, upended, with granite cliffs and deep, wide canyons. It had game because for untold centuries two-legged creatures had done little more than skirt its edges. Not until driven deep into it even the Indians hadn't really explored it and, as far as the soldiers who were sent to rout them out, it did not have a single redeeming factor, not even the shade during summer nor the crooked clear-water rivers, of which the largest was known as Lost River. It was the tributary of a dozen creeks, but after it entered the badlands it got lost among the deep canyons until

1

it eventually emerged somewhere far southward. Where settlers and soldiers found it down there, they called it the Rock River, probably because as far as anyone backtracked it, both sides were carved from solid rock.

It became Rock River after it reached the flatlands, the great plains which undulated for hundreds of miles with occasional bosques of trees, black and white oak, stalwart pines, and along the banks of the Rock River, almost impenetrable stands of willows.

All that open country was grassland as far and farther than a man could see. Thousands of buffalo had scarcely slowed its growth. With the buffalo gone, cattle taking their place, even over-grazing, the custom of cowmen, caused no lessening of the stirrup-high grass for two generations but, with the advent of the third generation, people accepted the fact that where it had once been possible to graze a critter on 100 acres, it now required a minimum graze of 300 to 400 acres, which created few difficulties to cowmen who'd matured accustomed to that much grassland per critter.

Near the easterly edge of this vast savanna was the town of Rock City. It had grown from a place where buffalo hides were piled sixty feet high until flatcars of the railroad came to take them east, to a cow town where, although the spur track remained and was still used, there was now a vast network of corrals for the transporting of cattle each autumn. The economy of Rock City flourished, because stockmen did not follow buffalo, they had roots and families, reasons to stay. Also, their vast holdings and big herds required more than just a shipping place for dry hides. They needed blacksmith shops, mercantile establishments, a physician, even an apothecary and a small dress shop, not to mention a harness works, a gun shop and a Southern Baptist church on the west side of the roadway near the entrance to Rock City from the north.

And a saloon which had once been a company shed for stacking buffalo hides to avoid getting them wet. There were some old gummers in Rock City who swore when it rained they could smell curing hides in the saloon, something the saloon's proprietor, a cigar-chewing Irishman named Michael Dougherty, stoutly denied.

Town Marshal Evan Stannard and the harness-maker, Frank Dennis, kept that story alive, not that either of them had ever detected the elusive scent but because it stirred the saloonman's ire.

Rock City was a cow town pure and simple, which meant that stockmen pretty much ordained how things should be, and that occasionally created a dilemma for Marshal Stannard, whose pay came in a roundabout way from an economy dependent upon ranchers. When he couldn't avoid it, he'd hold fire-eating riders overnight until they were sober, then send them on their way. It was customary to impose a two-dollar fine, which no one liked, particularly rangemen who worked for twelve dollars a month and found, and there had been protests, not just from the riders but also from their employers.

Marshal Stannard did not yield; either the rider or his employers had to kick in two cartwheels. It was, actually, a tempest in a teapot and while there were slightly strained relations between the lawman and the stockmen, generally the folks in town favoured Evan Stannard without saying so.

The blacksmith and wheelwright, a massive, tousle-headed man named Carl Edmunds got along well with just about everyone, but he did not care much for stockmen who brought him their damaged rigs and lame horses expecting miracles. That brought to a head, not the first confrontation, but what appeared to be the most serious one, when the hungover range boss of the Three Bells cow outfit look his saddle animal down to Edmunds' forge for new shoes all around and, while waiting, returned to the Irishman's saloon for some of the hair of the dog that had bitten him the night before.

Bells Ranch's head Indian was a lanky, weathered man called 'Tex' as was the custom for people out of Texas. He had a reputation for being hard, not just a hard drinker, but a rock-fisted brawler. The folks of Rock City avoided and tolerated him. For one reason the owner of Three Bells was a grizzled, unsmiling early settler who rarely smiled, never laughed, and thought only in terms of land and cattle. It was said he'd been married years back, which was probably true. Out at the Three Bells' big, tree-shaded yard there was a small, square piece of land encircled by an ornate iron fence where the only grave had a headstone bearing the name of Elizabeth Bovard, Beloved Partner of Samuel Bovard. It had no date of birth or death, but since Three Bells' owner was named Bovard — Samuel Bovard — it was, correctly, assumed Elizabeth had been his wife.

Sam Bovard owned several buildings in Rock City. He'd been around since the days of the hide-hunters, had taken up the best grassland with water rights, kept three riders year around and was known to back everything his range boss said or did.

When the range boss thought sufficient time had passed for his Three Bells' horse to be shod he returned to the smithy where the smith had a buggy wheel clamped in the wheelwright's rig. Tex Ordway found his horse out back dozing in tree shade, untied it, led it inside and noticed only its two front hooves had been shod. He lifted a rear foot to be sure he was right, then retied the horse, went over where the smith was applying different pressure to different parts of the buggy wheel, and tapped him on the back. When Carl Edmunds turned the range boss slammed him against the wheel rig and blessed him out. Edmunds straightened off the wheel rig, reached with a massive arm, pulled the range boss in close and knocked him senseless.

Across the road where the livery barn stood a swamper happened to be looking toward the open front of the smithy. When Edmunds struck the range boss, the swamper stood stock still with his mouth open. He eventually turned and yelled for his employer, Mark Wheeler, to come up front.

By the time the liveryman reached the roadway opening Edmunds had propped the range boss against a wall and was dousing him with water. The swamper said, 'He hit him, Mister Wheeler. I seen him hit him.'

The liveryman looked for something to sit on, found nothing handy and walked down the runway to a bench outside his office. He had known the smith five or six years and in all that time he had only once seen a man challenge him, and that brawl hadn't lasted long. Carl Edmunds was not only big, he had muscle crammed under his hide in places where most men didn't have hide.

When the range boss came around, Carl set him on a horseshoe keg and told him the stage company's yardboss had brought him that wheel the night before. As far as Edmunds was concerned he did work according to who came first. He then got a grey towel off a nail for the range boss to dry off with.

The range boss did not accept the towel nor say a word. His headache was back full force. He ignored Edmunds and everything else until he eventually went out back, got his horse and avoided riding up through town. He cut over behind the livery barn and headed for Three Bells in a slow lope, anything more jolting would have made his head hurt worse.

In a place no larger than Rock City what had happened at the smithy travelled like a brush fire. When Carl Edmunds, a single man, went up to the eatery after closing the shop for the night, the silence was deafening. Later, at the Irishman's saloon for a nightcap it was almost as silent, until Mike Dougherty asked if there'd really been a brawl at the smithy, or was it just another local yarn.

The blacksmith said exactly what had happened and the town marshal, farther along the bar, wearing a pained expression, leaned to consider Edmunds. 'Did you have to hit him?'

Carl also leaned when he replied, 'No, I could have called him a bullyin' son of a bitch. But that would have caused a fight too, wouldn't it?'

Nothing more was said until Edmunds left, heading for his quarters at the rooming-house, but plenty was said afterwards, and in general, while the lawman took no part, he privately agreed that it was about time someone yanked the slack out of the old man's mean-tempered range boss. Nevertheless he would have bet new money old Sam Bovard would show up in town breathing fire, and he didn't look forward to that.

The marshal's anxiety was pretty well shared by the residents of Rock City. The old man had raised hell a few times and had propped it up over the years when his riders, or himself, were even mildly slandered.

Frank Dennis, the harness man, cradled his beer glass in both work-scarred hands and said nothing as the discussion progressed, but when Marshal Stannard edged in beside him the harness-maker turned a solemn gaze and quietly said, 'That old man'n his riders is goin' to come boilin' into town faunchin' for trouble. Evan, it's been comin' for a long time. That old bastard's been ridin' roughshod over folks since I been here, an' that's close to seven years.' The harness-maker slapped a coin beside his empty glass, nodded and left the saloon.

For three days Rock City was a settlement where its inhabitants walked on eggs.

Evan Stannard visited the smithy, not once but twice. Each time the blacksmith retold the story the same way. He seemed the least worried, even though the paunchy liveryman across the road and his day man predicted something akin to the sky falling.

The marshal mulled over riding out to Three Bells to see if he couldn't salve things over. The reason he didn't make the ride was because old Sam Bovard and his range boss — two peas from the same pod — would stare him down in hostile silence. He'd had it happen before.

Something happened on the fourth day when a stranger arrived in town on the morning stage. Evan Stannard did not know him but a few old-timers did, but that scrap of information did not reach the marshal until along toward evening when he went to the café for supper and Mark Wheeler, the liveryman, who was short, balding, and heavyset, sat on the bench at the counter beside the marshal and quietly said, 'I never figured to see him again. He's been gone a good twenty years an' better.'

The marshal gave his order before facing the liveryman. 'What are you talkin' about?'

'The old man's son. Jim Bovard.'

Marshal Stannard stared. This was the first time he'd heard that Samuel Bovard had a son.

The liveryman nodded. 'Been at least twenty years. The way I heard it he left a few years after his ma died.' The liveryman snorted. 'That'd be understandable, wouldn't it?'

The marshal ate his supper thinking that the man who had left the Rock River country almost a quarter of a century ago might have hired a horse and gone out to Three Bells. He asked if this was the case and the liveryman shook his head. 'He come on the stage an' I seen him walkin' around town, but he didn't hire no horse from me. You want to see him? Try the rooming-house.'

Stannard tried Dougherty's saloon instead, which was where men congregated after supper. To ensure this clientele Dougherty had thought of putting in a poolroom out back, but that's as far it got.

When the marshal asked about Jim Bovard the saloonman stared. 'He's dead,' he stated. 'I heard that years back. Got shot somewhere in the California gold fields.'

That, of course, meant that the old man's son hadn't been in the saloon. Evan Stannard headed for the rooming-house, a ramshackle two-storey building at the north end of Rock City. On the way, with dusk settling, he encountered the harness-maker who was preparing to lock up for the day. Dennis jerked his head. The marshal followed him into the shop. Dennis closed the door and with his back to it said, 'You've heard of Jim Bovard?'

Stannard shrugged. 'I don't recollect, but today I have. Why?'

'I seen him this afternoon. Evan, he

hates the old man. I got no idea why but he does. I've heard enough stories about those two . . . '

'Frank, you can hear anything, but that was long ago.'

The harness-maker loosened a little. 'I can tell you somethin' I expect you ain't heard. Jim Bovard was gun guard on a stage up north. He deliberately shot an' killed two kids who tried to rob a stage. Shot each one four times.'

The marshal leaned on a counter. 'Gossip, Frank.'

'My cousin was the driver of that stage!'

The marshal hauled upright off the counter. He knew Frank Dennis as well as he knew anyone. He and the harness-maker shared a healthy scepticism about most things.

Dennis went behind the counter to his work table before speaking again. 'If Jim is back I think a man's got a right to be worried.'

For the lawman this discussion had

run its length. He left, walking in the direction of the rooming-house. Up there the crusty old man who ran the place with his equally cranky wife admitted that he'd rented a room to young Bovard but that was about all he said, except that he knew who he was and also knew he and his father hadn't been able to hitch horses for many years. The old man had no idea why Jim Bovard was back or, if he did have, he made no mention of it. The last he'd seen of the old man's boy was earlier when he'd gone in the direction of the eatery.

The marshal did not go to the café, he returned to his small office at the jailhouse, rolled a smoke, propped both feet atop the old battered desk and relaxed. Sooner or later he and Jim Bovard would meet; it was inevitable in a place no larger than Rock City, providing young Bovard didn't leave.

He was up at Dougherty's saloon when someone called from the roadway door that Sam Bovard had just entered town from the north with three riders. Dougherty and the marshal exchanged a look. As Stannard moved toward the spindle doors Dougherty groped for the shelf below his bar and brought forth one of the deadliest weapons west of the Missouri River, a shotgun which had been sawn off until both barrels were less than two feet in length.

The saloon's customers, four or five older men, crowded toward the solitary roadway window and watched. The townsman who had called out from the doorway had scuttled across the road as far as the leather works where he and Frank Dennis also watched from a roadway window.

News spread, folks who had been outside ducked inside. The general store's proprietor and his clerk had been in process of rolling some barrels of apples inside off the plankwalk; they left the last two barrels, went into the store where a pair of startled women shoppers stared until the storekeeper roughly told them Sam Bovard and his riders were entering town from the north. Nothing more was required to induce the woman to leave the store in haste. They were the only people in sight on either plankwalk, and they weren't in sight long.

Where Marshal Stannard was standing under the saloon's overhang, a man spoke quietly from behind him. 'It's time, Evan. It's past time for that old bastard to scare folks in town.'

The marshal neither responded nor took his eyes off the four riders one of whom was the rawhide-tough range boss. He rode with his tie-down thong hanging loose which normally was what kept his sixgun from getting jarred out of its holster.

The marshal's rack of weapons, including Winchester saddleguns, long barrelled rifles and three shotguns were at the jailhouse office. Whatever happened it was too late for him to cross over to his office.

Sam Bovard saw Stannard leaning in overhang shade and did not take his gaze off him as he came at a steady walk as far as the tie rack in front of the saloon, reined up and leaned on his saddlehorn without speaking. His riders lined up on both sides of him. One of them turned aside to expectorate and turned back as the old man spoke.

'We come to see the blacksmith. What he done to my foreman didn't have no reason.'

Evan Stannard returned the older man's gaze without blinking. 'Maybe, but I heard it different. He was cranky as a bitch wolf, an' this time he laid into the wrong man.'

The tobacco chewer expectorated again, otherwise there was a period of silence before the older man straightened up and raised his left hand to rein southward when he said, 'I never took kindly to folks here in town pickin' fights with my riders. You keep out of it.'

As the old man reined around and his three riders were doing the same, a third man emerged from a narrow dog trot between the saloon and the building southward and said quietly, 'Your range boss was lucky he picked on the blacksmith'n not me.'

The stranger was a spitting image of the old man, except that he was younger and darker. Sam Bovard's eyes widened as he stiffened in the saddle. After an interval he softly said, 'Boy, you better leave. You ain't welcome here.'

What happened next happened so swiftly, witnesses afterwards who were watching, had ten different versions they swore by. But two things were clear when the frightened horses reared, lunged, and fled back the way they had come leaving behind the tobacco chewer face down still clutching his unfired six-gun, and Sam Bovard struggling to arise holding an unfired and uncocked Colt.

For the space of what seemed an eternity the old man fought hard. No one moved nor spoke. His two remaining riders, with their horses finally under control, edged closer to the tie rack and one man dismounted and leaned to help the old man stand. Sam Bovard never made it, he died hanging half across the tie rack.

2

Bovard

A brindle dog that had been sleeping near the harness shop, sprang up and ran belly-down straight up the road until he disappeared.

Otherwise there was not a sound, not even after the echoes died. James Bovard paused to consider the dead tobacco chewer then growled at the rangemen supporting his father at the tie rack. They returned to their horses and mounted. Marshal Stannard approached the tie rack as the old man began to slide off it. When he landed on his back in the manured dust his son regarded him briefly, then picked up the old man's gun and shoved it in the front of his britches. He turned to face the utterly still onlookers as he said, 'Fair fight,' and walked southward.

Mike Dougherty leaned his scattergun aside to step ahead and consider the dead men. Three Bells' swarthy range boss said, 'Have the carpenter make boxes for 'em. We'll be back with a wagon.'

He and the town marshal exchanged a look before the range boss growled and led the other surviving man northward out of town at a dead walk.

The harness-maker walked over drying both hands on a faded apron, looked and said, 'Lay 'em in the shade. I'll send the carpenter for 'em.' Several men helped put the corpses in the shade of Dougherty's overhang as Frank Dennis went after the town carpenter.

Evan Stannard went down to the jailhouse, left the door open because it was hot inside, and was building a smoke when the goat-eyed proprietor of the general store came over. He had one blue eye and one brown eye. He was fat and pale with bulging eyes that watered. As he stood in the doorway he said, 'I didn't know who he was when he come in an' bought two cartons of handgun bullets.'

Evan considered the goat-eyed older man who was diffident by nature and an habitual worrier. 'Now you know, Mister Shepherd.'

'What started it? In the store it sounded like a war.'

'I'm not real clear about what started it but I'd say young Bovard didn't have no use for his pa.'

'He killed the old man?'

'The old man barely got his gun out. He killed one of the riders too. I don't recollect his name.'

'Marsha . . . four to one?'

'Mister Shepherd, I'd say five, six to one wouldn't have made much difference.'

'Did you talk to him?'

'Jim Bovard? No, but I will.'

'Marshal, it'll make folks uncomfortable havin' a gunman in town.'

'Makes me uncomfortable too,' the marshal replied, and watched the

24

merchant scuttle back across the road and disappear inside his store.

The elderly town carpenter had a long wheelbarrow he used for many things, including hauling dead people to his shop to be measured for coffins.

What had happened had occurred so fast and so unexpectedly that while Rock City's inhabitants discussed it, they did so in lowered voices and cryptically. It wasn't just the killings, but the passing of Samuel Bovard at the hand of his own son of all things, that would require changes, quite a number of them. For starters, who now owned Three Bells? If it was the old man's only son and heir, demonstrably a deadly man with a gun . . .

Tex Ordway and the other surviving Three Bells' survivor appeared the following morning with a light spring wagon. They stopped in front of the carpenter's shop, helped him load the coffins, drove out of town southward with their backs to all the watching eyes, turned westerly and kept on driving.

Not a word had been said to anyone but the carpenter and, as he recounted it at the eatery, all the range boss had said was how much he was owed for the boxes, paid him, and climbed on to the wagon seat and drove away.

The killing had been so sudden and unexpected the stunned residents of Rock City were unable to make an immediate adjustment, but as time passed several stories began to circulate. One which had originated among several old gummers who had been around during the heyday of Rock City hide trade, filled in the blank places and helped account for the twenty-year absence of the old man's son.

True or not, and there were a number of people who refused to believe it, the story was that Sam Bovard had caused his wife's death during a drunken rage. Regardless of the disagreeableness of Sam Bovard, no one cottoned much to the idea of a man doing such a thing. Nor did it help much that the old gaffers with whom the story had originated, were disreputable old racks of bones who lived in tar-paper shacks at the lower end of town.

Mike Dougherty in particular, denounced such an idea. Although he'd had no use for Sam Bovard, it was asking too much of him to believe old Sam — any man for that matter — would act that way toward female women

Marshal Stannard waited four days for James Bovard to show up in town. On the fifth day he saddled up and headed for Three Bells. It was a shot in the dark. After the gunfight Jim Bovard had checked out of the rooming-house and hadn't been seen in Rock City since.

It was the marshal's private opinion that the killer had left Rock City, but the corralyard boss for the stage company told Evan no one who even resembled Jim Bovard had bought passage on one of his stages, and it was this assurance that put Marshal Stannard in the saddle on the fifth day heading for the Three Bells' outfit.

The only person he mentioned his intention to was the saddle and harness-maker, Frank Dennis, who advised against riding out there alone.

Three Bells' yard was a fair distance westerly from town. Marshal Stannard struck out shortly after he and his horse had breakfasted. It was a beautiful day, the kind Evan Stannard would normally have enjoyed.

There were larks in the grass, busy digger-squirrels springing upright occasionally as they foraged, a large eagle making wide, gliding sweeps, and little bunches of wet cows grazing with calves at their sides.

Evan ignored all this. He knew the old man's range boss, Tex Ordway, was plumb loyal to the old man. He hadn't been in town since the shooting. Ornery as Ordway was, Evan Stannard did not believe he would be a match for young Bovard if push came to shove.

There were other questions the lawman wanted answers to when he topped out over the last long landswell and could see the Three Bells' yard. It was empty, which had no particular significance, the sun was high, rangemen would have ridden out shortly after breakfast.

A dog down in the yard either sighted or scented the lawman and barked. Several horses in a round pole corral south of the big old barn raised their heads, then returned to gleaning grass stalks in their dusty enclosure. Everything seemed normal to the marshal.

He urged his mount down the long-spending westerly slope and covered the distance to the yard without haste. He entered between two immense cotton-wood trees. The dog appeared from beneath the porch of the main house. He barked with one end and tentatively wagged his stub of a tail at the other.

When the lawman looped reins over the tie rack in front of the barn the dog, an overgrown pup, came corkscrewing and grinning. Evan leaned to scratch

29

his back, considered the main house with its old long covered porch, the log bunkhouse with the door ajar, and told the big pup he had an uneasy feeling, that someone ought to be around, and started across the yard toward the owner's residence.

The dog stayed at his side the full distance. Where they parted was where the dog ducked under the porch and the marshal climbed three broad steps and rattled the door with his fist.

His response was hollow echoes. He knocked three times then went to a hide-bottomed chair and sat down facing northward.

It did not trouble him much that this close to midday there was no one around. Stockmen loafed around a home place on Sunday, otherwise they rode, and this was not Sunday.

The dog came up to sit beside the chair and while Evan absently scratched its back he saw dust. He surmised riders were bringing in a gather, mostly marking and altering had been done months earlier, well before fly-time, but there were reasons for gathers. He and the big pup relaxed in porch shade watching the dust banner, which was coming toward the yard where a large network of pole corrals had been erected mostly southward of the barn but also behind it.

By the time he could make out cattle the pup abruptly left him and returned to its hidey-hole under the porch. It did not bark but watched intently as the distant shouts of riders reached the yard.

Evan arose to stand beside a porch upright. Mostly, the drive consisted of cows, but among them were a number of bulls, which was understandable; when stockmen wanted to bring in bulls they brought cows with them, otherwise they'd have one hell of a time trying to drive bulls by themselves.

The marshal had spent his early years working cattle. Everything he now watched fitted the custom of stockmen, except for one thing: when the drive was close enough for him to make out the riders, not a one of them was familiar.

That too, might have troubled him except for the fact that James Bovard's inheritance after the killing of old Sam and his tobacco-chewing rangeman, had been less than a week earlier and he had not heard in town of James Bovard hiring a new crew, something he certainly would have heard about.

The point rider saw a man on the porch, reined back to speak briefly with a man Evan thought was Jim Bovard. Right or wrong the point rider remained in the drag and the man he had spoken to reined out and around the gather heading for the yard in a lope. He bypassed the tie rack near the barn, and reined down to a walk as he crossed the yard. Evan recognized the old man's son and waited until Bovard halted near the steps, looped his reins and without nodding or speaking climbed the three broad steps.

When they were close Bovard said, 'You're a fair distance from home, Marshal.'

Stannard acknowledged that with a nod. 'Mind if we sit down?' he asked. The swarthy, powerful put-together unsmiling man made a gesture. 'You'll have some questions, I expect,' he said as he perched on the porch railing and thumbed back his hat.

Bawling cattle and shouting men were having difficulty corralling the cattle. Evan briefly watched this then asked his first question. 'Sore-footed bulls, Mister Bovard?'

The stocky man's dead-level dark eyes did not leave the lawman's face. 'No; cullin' the oldest ones.' Bovard then asked a question of his own. 'You know the livestock business, do you?'

'I did my share years ago,' Evan answered, looking at the other man, 'before I figured out there had to be an easier way to serve the Lord.'

Jim Bovard's features loosened in a

smile. 'You're right about that, for a fact. I grew up bustin' my butt on this ranch an' the same thought occurred to me many times . . . Marshal?'

'About your pa.'

'What about him?'

'Any brothers or sisters?'

Bovard's dark eyes narrowed. 'No. Just me. Is it the ranch you're interested in?'

'I guess not.'

'I hired a fee lawyer. He'll be along directly.'

'Was there a will?'

'Not that I've found an' I looked everywhere. If there had been the old son of a bitch would have left everythin' to a yeller dog before he'd leave it to me.' Bovard slid off the railing and resettled his hat. The drovers were having trouble with two large Durham bulls; they'd allowed themselves to be pushed as far as the gate but would not pass through.

'Marshal, I'll look you up in town in a day or two, but right now . . . '

Evan nodded as he also arose and watched the burly, dark man swing astride and ride toward the corrals where noise and dust was increasing by the minute.

When the lawman was astride he could see the two bulls defying the angry riders, rode his way down through the barn, hooked his horse hard and struck the nearest bull broadside. The bull went down, slobbered and trumpeted as he got upright. Marshal Stannard leaned as far as he could and swung his rawhide romal. It struck the bull on the nose. The bull whirled and ran into the corral. The second bull followed.

The marshal raised his right hand in a slight salute, rode back up through the barn, out into the yard and put his horse into a rocking-chair lope.

It was supper-time when he reached Rock City. After caring for his animal he went over to the eatery. The counter was nearly full. He took a seat at the farthest edge, nodded for supper and faced half around when the harness-man said, 'No trouble?'

'Nope. He'll be in directly. We had a little talk. Frank . . . ?'

'What.'

'Did you get a good look at him?'

'At Bovard? I seen him plain enough, why?'

'Did he look 'breed to you?'

'Maybe part Mex,' Frank Dennis replied.

With dusk thickening the marshal went to his office, cocked up his feet and eventually gave that up to go south of town and talk to some of the old men down there. Only one, old as dirt and toothless, offered anything even close to what the marshal wanted to hear, and all he said was, 'When he come to this country behind a gang of the measliest-lookin' bunch of slab-sided Texas cattle you ever seen there was two drivers an' a couple of In'ians. One was an old buck an' t'other one was a squaw who done the chores, drove his wagon. She chewed tobacco.

Them riders stayed about a year then quit to go home. I got no idea what become of the Indians, five, six years later he brought a woman to marry. Folks said she was from back East somewhere.' The old man paused to wipe a wet mouth before also saying, 'She upped an' died on him a long time ago. That's all I can tell you, Marshal. I don't recollect things much any more. Would you say this was worth a pony up at Dougherty's?'

Stannard gave the old man a paper dollar. It was enough to keep him bleary-eyed and incoherent for a week.

Two days later James Bovard appeared at the jail-house; he was either in a good mood or, just as likely, he had decided the town marshal wasn't a badgeheavy individual.

He took the chair near the door with a solid wall at his back and opened the conversation by informing Evan that his fee-lawyer had arrived and was in process of establishing James Bovard as legal heir to old Sam.

Evan accepted all this and offered Bovard a drink from a bottle from his lowest desk drawer and Bovard shook his head. 'Never could stand the taste of the stuff, Marshal.'

Evan put the bottle back in its dark place. Bovard watched all this from his relaxed position against the wall and when Evan kicked the drawer closed and raised his eyes the dark-eyed man said, 'It's a long story and I figure it's no one's business but my own. But I'll tell you this much. That old son of a bitch . . . '

'Your pa?'

'Yes. He had it comin' an' a whole lot more.' Bovard leaned forward holding his hat between his knees. 'I was years waitin' to do that. Now, I don't expect I can make folks like me, but I'll tell you flat out, they can or not as they please, but I'm here to settle among 'em.'

The swarthy man leaned back as though to arise when the marshal said, 'One question I'd like to ask you.

It's personal an' I really don't like to ask it.'

'Then don't, Marshal.'

'Did you shoot two kids tryin' to stop a coach?'

Bovard's eyes widened. 'Where did you hear that?'

'From a friend whose cousin was the driver of the stage.'

'Where did I shoot 'em, Marshal?'

'I think it was up north somewhere.'

'Well, you find out exactly where I did that an' I'll be back in the mornin' for the answer.'

Bovard slammed the door after himself and the lawman went to a small barred front window to watch him cross the road in the direction of the emporium. He waited several minutes then used the back alley to go up to the saddle and harness works. When he asked Frank Dennis to repeat the story of a highwayman shooting two youngsters four times each, Frank said it had happened on a run his cousin made between Fort Laramie and a stage stop known as Virginia Dale. 'Not too many miles south of the Colorado-Wyoming line.'

'How did your cousin know it was young Bovard, Frank?'

'He seen him plain as day. He grew up in the Rock City country, Evan. He knew Jim Bovard better'n I know you.'

For the lawman the riddle deepened. The following morning, early, James Bovard tied up out front of the jailhouse and caught Evan as he was heading to the café ready for breakfast across the road.

Bovard not only blocked the doorway, he used a rigid forefinger to push the marshal back from the door as he said, 'Where did I kill those highwaymen?'

'In that rocky country between Fort Laramie and a stage station called Virginia Dale.'

'When did I do that?'

'I don't know, but I guess it was four, five years back.'

Bovard jerked his head. 'Go sit

at your desk, I want to show you something.'

As the marshal returned to his desk and sat down, the muscular, dark-eyed man took some carefully folded papers from inside his shirt, spread the topmost paper open and held it that way with both hands as he said, 'Marshal, that's an army discharge. I served in the horse cavalry for six years. Read the damned dates. I spent them six years chasin' Messican raiders down along the border.' As he straightened up Bovard also said, 'I've never been in the Fort Laramie country in my life!'

3

A Big Country

When Stannard had read and reread the paper in front of him he looked up and leaned to arise as he said, 'Give me ten, fifteen minutes. I'll be back.'

Bovard got comfortable with his back to the front wall and waited for the marshal to return from the saddle and harness shop where Frank Dennis studied the army discharge, leaned back frowning and wagged his head. 'My cousin said he seen it happen plain as day.'

'When, Frank?'

'Well. Three years ago.'

Evan picked up the discharge and eyed his friend sceptically. 'Your cousin needs glasses,' he said, and marched back to the jailhouse where he handed James Bovard the discharge as he said,

'Folks make mistakes,' and sat down at the desk.

Bovard returned the paper to his pocket while eyeing the marshal. 'That kind of mistake can get a man killed.'

After Bovard departed Evan returned to the harness shop. 'Write your cousin,' he told Dennis. 'No need sayin' he was wrong, just ask him for all the details as he remembers 'em.'

Frank nodded and from habit wiped his hands on his apron. 'I expect he could be wrong, Evan.'

'I expect he could be,' the marshal replied and left the shop. The following evening when he was over at Dougherty's saloon he got a shock. Three young riders were bellied up to the bar drinking some of the dark beer Mike Dougherty made in his storeroom. The townsmen were accustomed to it. The general opinion was that Dougherty put in too much sugar. When it fermented it boosted the dark beer's alcoholic content high enough so that three glasses of the stuff would fry the *cojones* off a brass monkey.

The rangemen were young and they were strangers. The other customers exchanged surreptitious glances as the riders got louder after each glass of Dougherty's pride. Evan used the back-bar mirror to study the youths. When he figured they'd had enough he moved along the bar until he was close enough and shook his head at Dougherty, who was about to refill the glasses. Mike hesitated, looked from the flush-faced riders and back to the marshal, who held the saloonman's gaze. Dougherty reddened as he put the three empty glasses into the wash tub below the back-bar and used the cloth draped from his waist to make three large sweeps of the bartop where the younger men stood. He did not raise his eyes as he did this.

One of the riders, a gangling youth badly in need of shearing leaned to brush Dougherty's arm as he said, 'The refills, mister,' and Dougherty, who feared neither God nor the Devil, looked steadily back as he said, 'That's all, gents.'

The lanky rider frowned. 'You mean you don't have no more?'

Marshal Stannard spoke. 'You gents have had enough.'

The riders turned and Evan smiled. 'It's real stout beer.'

A short rider with the scraggly first growth of beard narrowed his eyes at the lawman. 'That ain't for you to say, mister.'

The saloon was fairly crowded but there was not a sound as the marshal spoke again. 'Gents, ride on home and sleep it off.'

That shorter, scraggly bearded youth stepped clear of the bar. As he did this he yanked loose the tie-down over his holstered Colt. 'Who the hell do you think you are?' he asked quietly.

'Marshal Evan Stannard.'

'The law?'

'Yep.'

'Well, Mister Law, you better crawl back in your hole. Us three ride for

Three Bells an' the way we heard it, Three Bells pretty well runs this country.'

'You heard wrong,' Evan said. 'Get astride an' go home.'

'Marshal,' the lanky youth in need of shearing addressed Evan. 'His name's Clint Bovard. His pa owns Three Bells. His pa won't take kindly to you pickin' a fight, an' if you know how fast his pa is . . . Clint's faster.'

Without a sound and almost without movement Dougherty lifted the scatter-gun from its shelf below the back bar, placed it facing the three younger men, and cocked it. The drunkest man west of the Big River sobered up fast looking down those twin barrels less than three feet away.

It was still enough to hear the lanky youth let out a long breath before he faced the shorter man as he said, 'Let's go,' and when the shorter youth did not move the third rider who was behind him, punched him in the back.

The Three Bells' riders left the saloon but Dougherty did not put the sawn-off shotgun back on its shelf until the sound of loping horses was audible.

Without raising his eyes, Dougherty went along his bar gathering glasses to be refilled and Evan Stannard loosened gradually and shoved his glass forward.

The town carpenter said what the others were thinking. 'Looks like we got a nest of gunfighters. Personally, I'd as lief have old Sam back.'

The following morning when Evan was unlocking the jailhouse door someone with very good eyesight tried to kill him from across the road down the north side of the emporium. What made the marksman miss by scant inches was the dark shadows that hadn't entirely dissipated from the west side of the road.

Evan dropped flat, gun cocked and ready. The only person visible was the blacksmith in his doorway attracted by the gunshot. He called up to

47

the marshal. 'I'll take the alley,' and disappeared back down through his shop.

Two old men moved cautiously toward the south end of the plankwalk and stopped. Evan got to his feet still holding the six-gun and crossed the road to pass down between the emporium and its neighbouring building to reach the west-side alley.

He met Carl Edmunds where the blacksmith was bent over frowning. Edmunds said, 'Tracks, Marshal, an' I can tell you one thing, I didn't shoe his horse.'

Frank Dennis and the saloonman joined them. The tracks led straight north out of town and there was not a horseman in sight.

They went back where the bushwhacker's horse had been tied. Judging by droppings the horse had been tied in one place for several hours.

Mike Dougherty said, 'That son of a bitch!' and the others looked at him. 'Well, gawdammit, by now the murderin' bastard's halfway back to Three Bells.'

No one commented although clearly Dougherty's statement satisfied them.

Evan returned to the jailhouse, stared at the fresh wound in the log wall inches from where his head had been, went inside, tossed his hat aside and got his bottle of pop-skull from the bottom drawer and swallowed twice.

It hit him like a mule kick. He went over to the café, endured the talk about the bushwhacking, got his horse and left town with a rising sun at his back heading west.

Frank Dennis and several others saw him leave, noted his direction and thought they should follow, keep out of sight but be handy when Evan reached the Three Bells' yard. They scattered to get their horses.

Evan Stannard had as much of a temper as any man had, but it rarely surfaced. Now, as he approached Three Bells' big yard he was mad enough to chew nails and spit rust.

He yanked the tie-down loose as he passed between the shaggy pair of cottonwoods and looked neither right nor left as he rode directly to the main house, dismounted, saw faces in the partially open bunkhouse door, climbed to the porch and struck the door with a rock-hard fist.

When James Bovard opened the door Evan punched him out of the way, stopped in the centre of the parlour and said, 'Where is he?'

'Where is who?'

'That gunfightin' kid of yours!'

Bovard was silent for a long moment before saying, 'How did you hear?'

'Hear what? Where is he?'

Bovard hung fire again before jerking his head and wordlessly leading the way to a dark bedroom where someone had tacked a blanket over the only window.

Evan stopped stone still. A tousle-headed stranger wearing trousers and a coat that matched looked up. Before the stranger could speak, if he'd intended to, Jim Bovard said, 'This here is my fee lawyer, Mister Tompkins.'

Evan neither looked at the lawyer nor acknowledged the introduction. He went to the side of the bed, considered the dark-eyed youth with the bandage around his upper body and spoke to the youth's father without taking his eyes off the boy. 'What happened?'

'Him an' my other two riders was returnin' from town last night. He got bushwhacked about a mile from the yard.'

Evan looked around. 'Last night?'

'That's what I said. I sent for a doctor, he bled like a stuck hog.'

Evan sat on the only chair and leaned. He and the youth exchanged a long stare before the youth hoarsely said, 'Was it you?'

Evan sat back. 'If I'd wanted to gunfight you I'd have done it in the saloon last night. What's your name?'

'Clinton. Folks call me Clint.'

Evan let out a long breath. 'Clint, some son of a bitch come within inches of blowin' my head off as I was unlocking the jailhouse this mornin'.'

For a long moment there was silence then the youth said, 'An' you come here because you figured I did it?'

'Somethin' like that.' Evan thumbed his hat back. 'I'd say there's someone don't like either one of us.'

The youth tried to smile, it was a feeble effort. His father brushed the lawman's shoulder and jerked his head. As they left the room the shockle-headed city man in matching britches and coat took the chair Evan had vacated.

Loud voices came from within the barn where the other Three Bells' riders were rigging out for the day's work. James Bovard pointed to a chair as he said, 'You any good as a tracker, Mister Stannard?'

'No. Are you?'

'Only after a rain.'

'The blacksmith in town's a good tracker.'

Bovard's face was drawn from anxiety.

'If I'd known . . . This gawddammed ranch is bad medicine, always was.'

Evan brushed that remark aside. 'Why would someone shoot your boy an' try to shoot me too?'

'It didn't have to be someone after both of you. My guess is that it was someone who don't like you. My boy . . . I've got enemies, Mister Stannard.'

Evan leaned forward watching the Three Bells' riders heading north-west from behind the barn as he said, 'If that was a coincidence I'm a monkey's uncle, an' Mister Stannard was my pa. My name's Evan.' He brought his gaze back to the swarthy man. 'How bad is the boy?'

'Through one corner of his lights on the right side. The doctor'll be here by tomorrow night.'

'What about the lads he was with?'

'He was in the middle.'

'That means the bushwhacker let them ride past. I didn't know you had a son. How about the other two?'

'Friends of his who wanted to

come along. They don't know much
. . . What you did when you rammed
that bull impressed the hell out of
them.'

'How well do you know them?'

'They're orphans. They lived with
me'n Clint.'

'Your wife, Mister Bovard?'

'Died birthin' the boy. We was both
young. Marshal, I want that son of a
bitch a thousand dollars' worth.'

Evan scratched the tip of his nose
and stood up. 'I'll backtrack'n try to
find where the lad was shot. If I find
the place I'll fetch the blacksmith to
do the trackin'.'

'I'll pay him five times what he'll
make as a smith. I'll get a horse an'
ride back with you.'

Evan shook his head. 'Don't leave
the boy. By the way, how old is he?'

'Fixin' to be sixteen.'

'Then he knew he wasn't supposed
to be in the saloon last night.'

Bovard cocked his head slightly.
'How old was you the first time?'

Evan smiled, nodded and left the porch, got his horse and rode without haste back the way he had come. He watched every yard of ground and if it had been an overcast day he'd have ridden by it, but sunlight reflects off brass better than off glass.

The casing had come from a .25-.35 gun, most likely a carbine, rangemen did not carry rifles.

The bushwhacker had used a narrow ravine to hide his horse. He had fired from between two large rocks. Evan was standing with his horse when it flung up its head. Evan watched three horsemen approaching. When they were close enough the harness-maker called out. He sounded and acted embarrassed.

Evan offered no greeting but held up the bullet casing which the three townsmen examined before handing it back. Evan said, 'Here's where Bovard's boy got shot last night.'

The townsmen were briefly silent. Evan said, 'It couldn't have been him,' and swung across leather to lead the way back to Rock City. Dougherty rode a full mile darkly frowning before he asked a question. 'The same son of a bitch, Evan?'

'Most likely not. He'd have had to ride like hell to be in town before sunrise, an' where his horse was tied there was a lot of droppings.'

Rock City was alive with rumours. When the marshal and his companions returned, people watched them go as far as the livery barn, did not go down there but gathered in small groups elsewhere. Later, when they heard that Bovard's son had been shot the previous night, their best conjectures went out the window and it would be a while before new ones would appear.

Mark Wheeler, the liveryman, was across the road at the smithy when the marshal appeared. He remained in shadows and heard the lawman talking with the smith about the other shooting and ask for Edmunds' help tracking the lad's bushwhacker. As soon as the marshal departed, the liveryman went up to the saloon to repeat what he had learned by eavesdropping.

By the following morning folks around Rock City knew as much as their lawman knew. They were prepared when the marshal and the blacksmith left town with the sun barely rising, heading in a direction which was slightly northward and mostly westerly.

Because of his size and heft the blacksmith rode a large pudding-footed horse that weighed close to 1,400 pounds. Both Edmunds and his horse were recognizable for some distance. Fourteen hundred pound horses wore collars that pulled things. No rangeman in his right mind would be caught dead straddling a horse that large and unhandy.

It could be said in the large horse's favour that he had a long stride, never slackened and responded to the slightest touch of the reins.

By the time his rider and Marshal Stannard reached the spot where the .25-.35 casing had been found the sun was climbing and visibility was perfect. Edmunds dismounted, walked slowly in a large circle, found where the horse had been tied prior to the bushwhack, and stood a long time gazing northward before striking out on foot leaving the large horse to be led by the marshal. Edmunds did not speak until the climbing sun was approaching its apex, then he sashayed toward a piddling little warm-water creek and there, for the first time, Evan Stannard saw the tracks where a rider had dismounted and stood with his animal as it tanked up. There was the customary verge of greenery on both sides of the creek, the ground was warm and soft.

Edmunds groped for a plug, gnawed off a corner, spat into the water and said, 'Whoever he is, he knows the country,' and raised a massive right arm. 'See that field of rocks yonder with the trees among 'em? My guess is that's where he made a stop to watch his back trail.'

They splashed across the creek, approached the rocks and trees without Edmunds looking at the ground. Shortly before they encountered the first boulders he dryly said, 'If he's up there it'd be like shootin' pigeons in their loft.'

He wasn't there but he had been. Several stubs of brown paper cigarettes showed where the bushwhacker had killed them. Evan scratched his head. 'It was dark, Carl. Why would he worry about someone followin' him?'

The blacksmith shrugged. 'Don't make sense for a fact,' he replied and started ahead reading sign that the marshal saw only as an occasional disturbed small rock.

Edmunds stopped again among the scrub oaks where there was shade. 'You know this country?' he asked.

'Sure don't but like you said he does.'

Edmunds faced the lawman. 'It's open territory ahead. We'll be visible an' he won't have to be very savvy to know we're trackin' him. You want to keep goin'?'

Evan studied the country. As far as he could see there were other small bosques of trees, otherwise as the large man had said, it was open grassland.

Edmunds spoke again. 'Sure as Gawd made green grass he's up ahead an' my guess is that he's watchin'. He'd know shootin' that feller, there be a hunt on for him. It's up to you, Marshal, but me'n my horse make big targets.'

The blacksmith clearly wanted to turn back. Evan told him to head back, that he'd push on a few miles farther.

The blacksmith squeezed the big horse and without another word continued tracking. Without saying it he was convinced that sooner or later they would fit into the buckhorn sights of an ambusher.

With the sun standing directly overhead they saw a rider, and long before the marshal made the distinction Edmunds said, 'A woman.'

60

They altered course to reach one of those clumps of oaks, moved into the speckled shade and dismounted. Edmunds was intrigued. 'She's comin' straight for us. You don't expect she'd be the bushwhacker, do you?'

Evan leaned beside a tree watching the oncoming rider. He had no idea about her being the bushwhacker. In fact he'd never heard of a female woman setting up a bushwhack.

Edmunds interrupted the lawman's reverie. 'She's young. Can you see her?'

'Yeah.'

'Did you ever see her before?'

Evan shook his head. 'Not that I recollect.'

'Maybe she lives hereabouts.'

Evan scotched that. 'We been on Three Bells' range all mornin' an' we're still on it. The only folks livin' here are the Bovards.'

The woman sat her horse with perfect balance. Whoever she was, one thing was certain: she'd been straddling saddle animals a long time.

Evan straightened up. 'Stay hid,' he told the blacksmith. 'If she's bait for another bushwhack I'll feel better with you watchin' my back.'

Edmunds clearly made out details and spoke his thoughts when he said, 'She's pretty as a speckled bird, Marshal. She wouldn't be part of a bushwhack.'

Evan moved toward the first tier of trees and waited, and for a fact the blacksmith was right. She was young with severely drawn-back red hair. Her features were even and as she rode toward the marshal she smiled.

He stepped clear of shadows and when she stopped with both gloved hands atop the saddlehorn she said, 'Good morning. I didn't expect to see anyone out here. My name is Lee Bovard.'

That shocked the townsmen. Evan offered a hand but she did not dismount. He asked the obvious question and she answered it without hesitation.

'I'm James Bovard's niece. My mother was his sister.'

Evan said exactly what he thought. 'I've never heard Mister Bovard had a sister.'

Her smile lingered. 'Are you the town marshal from Rock City?'

'Yes'm, an' the big feller is the town's blacksmith, Carl Edmunds.' Evan thought her smile was beautiful, which it was. He asked how young Clint was and her smile faded. 'My uncle is frantic waiting for the doctor. I had to get away, for a while anyway. Marshal . . . ?'

'Trackin' the bushwhacker, ma'am.'

She twisted from the waist and raised her right arm. 'The tracks lead straight into a lava bed of glass rock.' She faced forward. 'If his horse had been bare-footed he'd possibly have left no sign, but it was shod. You can pick up the trail. It goes northerly toward that rough country where the river comes out.' She rested both hands atop the saddlehorn looking down at him.

'Are you familiar with this country, Marshal?'

'No ma'am.'

'Neither am I but *he* is. By now he's most likely sitting atop one of those peaks up yonder watching.' She smiled again, this time including the blacksmith. 'Good luck, Marshal. Be careful.'

She reined around, boosted the chestnut gelding into a smooth lope in the direction of the Bovard yard.

The men she'd left behind were like statues until she grew small in the distance, then Edmunds softly said, 'Prettiest woman I ever seen. How about you?'

Evan avoided a direct answer. 'How 'n hell did she know the bushwhacker went north?'

'By his mark.'

'Did you ever know a woman tracker, Carl?'

'No, but that's one I'd give a lot to go trackin' with.'

Evan considered the forbiddingly

dark and twisted northward country, got his horse, mounted and without another word led the way back toward Rock City. Several miles along he turned. 'I'll be double-damned,' he said quietly, and the blacksmith agreed. 'Me too.'

4

A Discovery

The physician arrived on the late-day stage, hired a horse at Wheeler's barn and followed Wheeler's direction to reach the Bovard place.

The liveryman wasted no time telling the marshal a doctor had hired a horse from him and had ridden toward the Bovard place. The marshal's office wasn't the only place Wheeler carried his story, Mike Dougherty's clientele heard too, as did the saloon-man.

When the physician did not return after two days, local speculation ran wild. Marshal Stannard was concerned but what really intrigued him was the stunning woman he and Carl Edmunds had met, Lee Bovard. He wanted to ride to Three Bells but couldn't come up with a good excuse.

It wasn't just Lee Bovard as a female woman that Evan wondered about, it was her tracking ability. He had never before even heard of a woman who could read sign unless it was after a heavy rain and the critter to be tracked had feet like an elephant.

The morning of the third day the local corralyard boss for the stage company came breathlessly to the jailhouse to inform Evan the southbound morning stage from Dennison had been stopped and the passengers robbed down to the finger rings by two unshaven, unwashed men who seemed willing to kill even the female passengers.

Evan got directions, rounded up a posse and left town despite the strong possibility that dusk would descend before they reached their destination.

They made good time and eventually arrived where the robbery had occurred, and they found tracks but dusk's inevitable arrival ended the manhunt. On the ride back it was said that, since the tracks seemed to be heading for the rugged northerly country, finding the highwaymen might prove to be not only difficult but dangerous. Before the whites, Indians had used the wild rims to discourage pursuit after raids.

When the possemen split up after returning to town Evan lighted a lamp in his jailhouse, sat down and vigorously scratched while accepting the fact that the rugged and wild north country would be ideal for outlaws to hide in and rousting them out, even finding them, would be nearly impossible.

He was leaning to turn up the lamp mantle when it occurred to him that the bushwhacker of Clinton Bovard had headed in the same direction. He leaned back after achieving more light and told himself there didn't have to be a connection; renegades of any kind would see that rugged country and naturally head for it.

He was preparing to lock up for the night when another thought occurred, and he dismissed it out of hand. Maybe the highwaymen belonged to a party including the bushwhackers.

It was, he told himself, reaching pretty far to entertain such a notion, but when he was bedding down at his boarding-house room, he was kept awake by another thought. Whoever had tried to kill him and whoever had shot James Bovard's son and had stopped the stage, whose tracks led in the direction of the primitive north country, just damned well might have a connection. It could be a gang. If he found evidence of that, and if a band of them were in the wild country, they'd leave tracks. If that were so and if he found sign it just might indicate that at least one of them was familiar with the rugged north country, and he could count on the fingers of one hand the number of men who had explored that country, which should make it possible for him to narrow the identity of the renegades.

It was all guesswork, but when the marshal arose in the morning to go out back and clean up in

69

cold spring water, he told himself that with nothing else, he might as well do a little horsebacking. After breakfast where community arousal over the stage robbery had for the time being superseded other topics of interest, he listened to the talk and was paying the caféman when a stranger who wore glasses as thick as the bottom of a whiskey bottle, said, 'They got my sample case and nine dollars.' Someone asked the drummer what was in the sample case and when he replied there was a moment of silence, then uproarious laughter.

'Ladies undergarments trimmed with real lace.'

The drummer was not amused. Over the noise he also said, 'Their faces were covered but I'll never forget one of them. He had a leather belt holding up his britches. It had a silver buckle with a horse on it in gold, and the belt where it went around him had silver squares with silver buttons between.'

The marshal left town by the north

alley. He did not particularly want a volunteer along, this was going to be a long, arduous and tiring ride. He did not expect to return until well after dark.

The Rock River country was for miles flat to rolling with very little shelter. Except for the arrow-straight stage road and the village at its southerly end, the territory was little altered from Indian times, except for the absence of buffalo.

After passing the robbery site the marshal quartered until he found the tracks again and with dazzling daylight resumed where he and his possemen had had to give up the previous night.

It was a tedious process because Evan Stannard was not an accomplished tracker. At one particular clearing where sign was clear, he wished he might encounter the handsome dark-eyed woman again.

There was no question about the destination of the highwaymen, they took the shortest route into the primitive country and the last mile before entering the timbered and densely brushed uplands, he made no attempt to follow sign.

Where the river was squeezed between a pair of high bluffs it sounded like continuous thunder. Evan picked up shod horse sign where the soil was spongy, satisfied himself the highwaymen were not going to change course for an excellent reason, not even horses with wings could get out of the canyon, and spent less time watching tracks and more time eyeing the endless array of dark places where an ambusher could have watched him cross into the uplands.

Whether he encountered anyone or not, he was satisfied that whoever he was seeking specialized in bushwhacking. Once, when his horse missed a lead and threw up its head, its rider yanked loose the thong that prevented his sidearm from falling out of its holster.

He rode slowly, the only moving creature he saw was a high circling buzzard. If he'd been an Indian he would have read significance into this sighting. Being a non-Indian not given to interpreting omens, the hair on the back of his neck nevertheless stood up.

What the horse had seen or scented was a large doe with a spotted fawn. They had come to drink and only saw the rider when they had tanked up and the doe stood motionless for a brief moment, then snorted and led her baby in a sprint for the nearest dark tangle of undergrowth.

The horse wanted to drink so the first eddy above where the deer had been that offered quiet water, Evan swung down, removed the bridle and let the horse fill up. As he was leaning beside the horse several crows abruptly appeared making a raucous racket as they flapped frantically eastward. The marshal backtracked their flight to a small gathering of pines and oaks.

Sunlight bounced off metal up there. Evan rebridled and walked on the far side of his horse until he was sheltered from whoever was higher up, then left the animal tethered to a sour apple tree, took his Winchester and used it to break a passage northward. Twice he ventured closer to the river. The first time he saw the reflection again, but the second time it did not appear.

He had to guess that the sentry up yonder had left his post to carry the message of Evan's coming. Whether he might have recognized the lawman was problematical, but that wouldn't matter to fugitives. Anything and everything threatened them.

Unable to cross the river lower down, he worked his way alongside it northward until he found a very wide place where the water was not roiled, where huge old slippery, ancient boulders showed above the water and safely made a perilous crossing. His boots were soled with leather. Once soaked it offered no help; he had to reach the far shore by maintaining perfect balance, which he was able to do by using the saddlegun as a balancing tool.

The west bank had even more dense underbrush. It also happened to have an ancient trail through solid rock, something which was not as bizarre as it seemed. That quiet-water pool would have provided early inhabitants of this country with an ideal place to spear and snare fish, probably for centuries.

He followed its bends, loops and sashays around nearly perpendicular granite walls where birds had nests in holes and flew above him.

The sun had passed its meridian before he topped out and sat down to suck air while examining the big plateau. It had no trees and only the hardiest varieties of brush and grass for an excellent reason, the soil was no more than three inches deep, below that there was solid granite.

As well as he could discern he was alone. Because people who rode horses made notoriously poor walkers and hikers, the marshal sat in one place chewing jerky and gauging the area in three directions. Directly below was the river canyon.

Eventually he began a methodical search for the place where that sentinel had been, and finding it did not prove difficult. Not only had the man left brown paper cigarette stubs but his horse had left enough evidence to suggest its rider had been in his high place for several hours, perhaps most of the morning and part of the afternoon, until he had seen a rider enter the canyon.

This time the tracks were more difficult to read; the horse making them had not been shod.

He ignored the passage of time, especially when he cut sign of several riders going north-east deeper into the wilderness.

He located their camp and read as much as he could from it. If he'd been an Indian — or a handsome dark-eyed woman — he could have read more, but finally when he glanced over his shoulder he saw the position of the descending sun and started back to find the river canyon trail.

He was satisfied that he had found the camp of highwaymen. In fact, from where the watcher had been positioned, it was possible to see the stage road.

His horse had waited impatiently and nickered when it heard him coming. The animal drank one more time then, knowing in which direction it was being ridden, lengthened its stride. Horses, unlike cows, had no stomach to store forage to be rechewed for close to ten hours before it saw the lights of Rock City through a night of velvet darkness.

Evan slept like a dead man. What awakened him the following morning was someone knocking on the door of his room with a powerful fist.

He yelled for the visitor to be patient, stepped into his britches, shrugged into his shirt and was about to stamp into his boots when an angry man cursed a blue streak and struck the door again, this time hard enough to rattle the entire wall.

Evan held the gun behind his back as he opened the door and James Bovard hurled himself past it and glowered. 'Where'n hell was you all day yestiddy?' And before the marshal could reply Bovard said, 'They stole close to a hunnert head, cows, steers and bulls. Cut 'em out up north where they wouldn't be missed, but my niece rode up that way, read the sign and rode back to tell me. Mister Stannard, I'm goin' to hang 'em from trees an' leave 'em hangin' until they rot!'

Evan crossed to the peg holding his shellbelt, swung it into place, leathered the gun he'd been holding and said, 'How long ago, Mister Bovard?'

'We got to guess; nobody goes miles northward except to gather an' the last time anyone made a gather was early last spring. But Mister Stannard, you can't drive a hunnert head without leavin' a trail. It's not like stealin' horses. Cattle can't run.'

Evan hadn't cleaned up or eaten. He told the swarthy man to wait for him at the jailhouse and handed Bovard the key.

He cleaned up out back and dried himself on the ancient towel which most of the time hung dolorously on a nail near the pitcher and wash basin.

At the eatery most of the diners had eater earlier; the ones left were corralyard swampers and a couple of the old gummers from south of town. The caféman brought the marshal's platter, refilled his coffee cup and said, 'Amos was lookin' for you yestiddy.'

The lawman finished, paid up and went out into the sunbright roadway. The storekeeper's clerk saw him and called back to his employer as Evan was crossing toward the jailhouse.

There was no interception although there could have been if Shepherd hadn't been so diffident by nature. He followed Evan into the jailhouse and as Evan was lowering himself into the chair at his desk he said, 'Mister

Bovard come to town yestiddy raisin' hell an' proppin' it up because you wasn't to be found.'

Evan jutted his chin Indian-fashion in the direction of a chair as he said, 'I talked to him this morning. He's been raided by rustlers.'

The paunchy merchant with the wet eyes rolled one edge of his half-length apron in both hands as he also said, 'He should have kept Tex Ordway on as range boss. He knew Three Bells better'n even old Sam. No one would have run off cattle when the old man's range boss was around, an' he's back.'

'Who is back?'

'Tex Ordway.'

Evan sat a little straighter in his chair. 'How do you know that, Amos?'

'I seen 'em. I was takin' a load of supplies out to the Bridger place and . . .'

'When?'

'Day before yestiddy. As I was sayin', I seen him an' another feller passin' northward on the stage road. When I come out of a ravine they was lopin' northward off the road.'

'How do you know it was him?'

'Marshal, I see good. I'd know that disagreeable bully as far as I seen him, an' it wasn't far. Just before I followed the Bridger road down into that ravine, I seen him plain as day.'

'Did you know the other feller?'

'Not that I can recollect. He was sort of wiry and set a horse like he was born on one.'

Evan kept the discussion going until the merchant was beginning to repeat himself, then got rid of him.

He sat back staring at the far wall entertaining some interesting and uncomplimentary thoughts. Ordway was a vicious, venomous individual. Evan had locked him up to sober up the night before the blacksmith cleaned his plough, and Ordway knew all that north Bovard range right up to where it met the Rock River canyon and most likely the wild country northward. He did not like the marshal. He did not like James Bovard for replacing him and he probably resented the Bovards not just because of old Sam's killing but also because he'd worked years for old Sam and likely expected something better than being abruptly fired by old Sam's son. It was even possible old Sam and Tex Ordway might have had some kind of agreement of reward for Ordway serving the old man so well for so long.

The more Stannard sat staring at the wall the more reasons he found for suspecting that wherever Ordway had gone after being fired, his return to the Rock River country was motivated by revenge against the Bovards and hatred for the lawman, and that would almost certainly extend to the blacksmith who had given him a shellacking. It was common knowledge that Ordway was a hater.

The marshal was staring at the wall, hands clasped behind his head when James Bovard walked in out of the hot sunlight. He barely nodded and said nothing until he'd taken the chair Amos Shepherd had recently vacated.

If he'd come to talk he did not get a chance. Marshal Stannard quietly informed him that the old man's range boss was back and explained his thoughts and suspicions. It took the better part of a half-hour to get it all said, and during that time the swarthy man resettled himself twice in the chair. When the lull came he said, 'My lads are trackin' the cattle,' and that brought Marshal Stannard straight up in his chair. Tracking a hundred cattle would be as easy as falling off a log. He said, 'Mister Bovard, those are boys. Two boys. Whoever drove off your cattle aren't boys, they're men who'd as lief kill boys as pick ticks off a horse. That many cattle being driven off their home range can't be driven by two men. If Tex Ordway is along that'll be three, an' I got a feelin' there's at least three.'

Bovard sat loose and sprawled as he

said, 'Mister Stannard, we got no idea when they rustled those cattle, but it wasn't yestiddy nor the day before. Those boys won't even get close for a couple of days.'

The marshal arose. 'Are the boys good sign readers?'

'They wouldn't have to be as long as my niece is with 'em.'

Evan stared at the other man. 'The girl, your niece? She's with them?'

'Yes. She can track flies across a glass window.'

Evan sank back down. 'Could she guess ahead, Mister Bovard?'

'Most likely, yes. There are things driven cattle got to have, water, graze an' rest. She knows that.'

Evan flushed. 'You're crazy to let that girl go after cow thieves! An' two greenhorn boys. You're goin' to have nightmares the rest of your life if those rustlers know they're being follered and believe me, rustlers keep watch down their back trail. They'll set up an ambush sure as we're settin' here.'

James Bovard arose. 'I come to town to round up some men to ride with me. We'll meet Lee an' the lads an' take it from there. Marshal, I got four riders. I don't want you along.'

Evan dryly said, 'Leave 'em hangin'?'

Bovard nodded and left the jailhouse office.

5

A Chance Encounter

Up at the saloon Mike Dougherty confirmed that James Bovard had hired four townsmen to ride with him. He said when they caught up he'd pay an extra five dollars if they'd lean with him on the ropes when they caught some cattle thieves.

Mike tossed aside the cloth he usually wore tucked into his trousers for wiping his bar. Without asking he said, 'I'll fetch Frank. The three of us ought to be enough.'

The marshal returned to the doorway, watched Dougherty cross over and enter the harness shop. He went south to get his horse and a booted Winchester which he was buckling into place beneath his right saddle fender when Dougherty and Frank Dennis appeared. They too had booted saddle guns. Neither of them owned a saddle animal so they went down to Wheeler's barn and hired mounts.

Mark Wheeler watched as the carbine boots were tucked into place without saying a word until the animals were being led out front to be mounted, then all he said was, 'Take care of my horses.'

Neither man answered as they rode toward the jailhouse where the liveryman saw them meet the town marshal after which the three of them rode up out of town on the north-south stage road.

Dougherty had locked the saloon, which frustrated the liveryman so he went to the general store to say what he had just witnessed. There was only Amos and his elderly clerk with the black sleeve protectors; there were no customers, so Wheeler's bit of gossip did not get the broad reception it usually got at the saloon.

The storekeeper already knew about Bovard being raided, which had upset him, but this latest scrap of information sent Amos Shepherd to the counter display of both red and blue bandannas to select one and dab at his bulging eyes with it.

Most of the summer was gone, including the heat which pretty well kept folks indoors. Now, as the lawman and his companions left Rock City behind, oncoming autumn was more than a promise; early as it was, trees were shedding, little groundswell breezes brought cold air and it was the time of year when stockmen began gathering for the cut and the long drive to rails' end and the large assortment of corrals the top stringers of which were six feet from the ground.

When the marshal and his companions reached the place where the stage had been stopped, Frank Dennis said, 'The corralyard boss has been raisin' hell.' Dougherty took this up. 'He told me last night the stage office up in Denver's lookin' for reasons to cut back.'

Evan picked up the gait; for several

miles they loped. Evan did this several times. When the harness-maker said his seat wasn't used to hard saddlebacking, the marshal replied shortly, 'Frank, I'd like to get far enough north to cut westerly an' maybe sight Bovard.'

Dennis did not complain again, but when his friends were occupied elsewhere he stood in his stirrups.

The territory roughened on both sides of the road. When they were nearing the cut between high banks where the road levelled off for about half a mile, the marshal said, 'Frank, if you'd stole a band of cattle which way would you drive 'em?'

Dennis answered promptly. 'South as far an' as fast as they'd go. Messico's a prime market for stole cattle.'

Evan hadn't expected that answer. For a while, until they reached the topout after which the road went downhill, he halted. 'They didn't use the road,' he muttered and Mike said, 'You didn't expect them to, did you?'

The marshal looked for and found

a dim trail going west and when he reined toward it the harness-maker groaned. They would be riding into and across some of the most rugged, inhospitable land on earth.

The sun was slanting away before Evan halted at a brush-choked creek that seemed to come out of pure rock. Dougherty dismounted to water his animal and gazed dispassionately at the marshal. 'What're you tryin' to do, get ahead of Bovard?'

Evan nodded and the saloonman's scowl deepened. 'Evan, ain't Bovard nor anyone else, let alone thieves with cattle, goin' to be in this gawdforsaken area.'

The marshal raised up from drinking, wiped his chin and said, 'Three chances, Mike. For a damned fact there's outlaws up in here somewhere. They robbed the stage an' I'll bet you new money they tried to bushwhack me in town, an' did bushwhack Bovard's boy.'

Dougherty wagged his head. 'I thought

we was lookin' for rustlers.'

They rested the horses for a while then resumed their westerly way with the sun off-centre and shadows beginning to puddle where there were stands of giant fir trees.

Without warning as they sashayed clear of dense timber a big cow elk almost ran into them. Her eyes were wild and her tongue was out.

They stopped. She hadn't been running as though from an insistent bull elk. They dismounted, got their carbines and were ready when the mounted hunter came in flinging pursuit, carbine held high. He did not see the three men until Evan sprang astride and lunged to block his way, then the hunter hauled back instinctively to avoid a collision and stared. That was when Mike snugged back his carbine and said, 'Drop the gun!'

The hunter's surprise was complete as Frank Dennis left his horse, walked forward, grabbed the hunter by the shirt and yanked him out of the saddle. The hunter lost his carbine in the fall. Evan's eyes narrowed at the grounded hunter as he told Frank to get the hunter's six-gun. As Frank moved to do this the hunter tried to scramble to his feet. Frank hit him under the ear, emptied the holster and shook his head at the dazed man. 'You could break a horse's leg ridin' in rocky country like you was doin'. Get up!'

As Frank hoisted the wiry man upright Evan said, 'What's your name?'

The wiry man was dark and lined from exposure. He had pale eyes and hair streaked with grey. Frank shook him hard before he answered the lawman. 'Bart Smith. Who the hell . . . what the hell you doin' up in here?'

Evan had another question. 'Where's Ordway?'

'Who?'

Evan went closer. 'Mister, you rode with Tex Ordway a few days back.'

'I don't know what . . . '

Evan interrupted. 'If I didn't want folks to remember me I wouldn't wear a belt with silver conchos around it nor a buckle with a horse overlaid on it. Where is Ordway? Mister, we're in a hurry.'

Frank cocked a fist. Dougherty used the hunter's carbine when he jammed the barrel into the man's soft parts.

'He ain't nowhere around here,' the wiry man said from a doubled-over position.

After a moment the marshal said, 'Get on your horse an' lead us to your camp.'

Dougherty took both reins as the wiry man got astride. He grinned at him. 'You're pretty close to the end of your rope. If you're real lucky you'll be real careful. That big feller on the horse behind you'll blow you in half. Lead off, you son of a bitch.'

The captive hadn't entirely recovered from being waylaid in a part of the wild uplands where he had reason to believe there were no people. He was short, likely didn't weigh 150 pounds with rocks in his pockets, had a weasel's close-set eyes and a cruel lipless mouth. As he gave Frank Dennis directions he seemed less fearful than frantic. They were weaving in and out among mammoth old firs when he addressed Evan Stannard. 'You from Rock City?' When Evan nodded he asked another question. 'You know the lawman down there?'

Evan hung fire before answering. 'I am the lawman down there, an' you're the son of a bitch who tried to bushwhack me, aren't you?'

The wiry man yanked straight up in his saddle. 'I never met you before in my life an' that's the gospel truth.'

Dougherty said, 'Lyin' bastard. Evan, we can find their camp. Let's hang this carrion an' get it over with.'

Evan halted. Frank and Mike did the same. None of them carried a lass rope but the wiry man had one under the right-hand swell of his saddle. He spoke swiftly as he ran the words together.

'I'll tell you what you want to know. It wasn't me shot Bovard's boy. It was Hiram, an' it was Tex hisself who hid out in Rock City to kill you, Sheriff. He hates your guts.'

'I'm a town marshal, not a sheriff,' Evan replied. 'Who is Hiram?'

'Hiram Bullinger. Him'n me been partners a long time. He's . . . '

'Is he in the camp you're takin' us to?'

'I expect so. By now he should be back. Him'n Tex got the cattle lined out. I stayed with 'em until we was sure. Tex is goin' to meet the buyer westerly across this bad country. Hiram's supposed to come back an' scout up Bovard's horses so's when Tex gets back we can round 'em up.'

Mike Dougherty eyed the wiry man calling himself Bart Smith. If he was telling the truth, and he seemed too frightened not to be, there was no way Evan and his companions could reach the stolen cattle before Bovard did. He had to hope very hard that the girl and her pair of young riders hadn't ridden into an ambush by now. He asked the wiry man if they'd watched their back trail while driving the stolen cattle.

'Sort of,' he replied. 'Them cattle didn't drive worth a damn. It took all three of us to keep 'em together. Tex rode back a few times an' once Hiram climbed a hill. There was no one in sight down the back trail.'

Evan nodded and Dougherty rattled the reins to get the captive's horse to strike out.

Daylight still shone brightly in flat country but where the men from Rock City were riding, even on the brightest days it was gloomy and as this particular day passed the gloom was beginning to deepen.

The wiry man held up a hand. They halted. He was peering ahead when he spoke in a lowered voice. 'There's a creek an' a little clearin'.'

'How far?'

'Half-mile, thereabouts.'

Frank dismounted, handed his reins

to the saloonman, yanked out his carbine and went ahead. Evan and Dougherty dismounted. Mike pulled their prisoner from the saddle. As he touched down he said, 'All's I done was hire on with Tex.'

'Lyin' bastard,' Mike growled. 'An' helped steal a herd of cattle, an' snuck around in the dark to bushwhack someone.'

'No! As Gawd's my witness, Tex an' Hiram left me in camp when they went down yonder. Hiram was supposed to kill Bovard. Tex was supposed to kill the marshal. Hiram said he killed Bovard.'

'What'd Tex say?'

'That he missed you but was goin' to make sure the next time.'

Dougherty had a question. 'You 'n Hiram stop that coach an' rob the passengers?'

The wiry man ran a nervous hand over his unshaven face and avoided looking at the saloonman. 'Tex was mad as hell. He didn't want anythin'

97

to happen until we got the cattle. He cussed us out good. He didn't want no one to know he come back here.'

Frank Dennis firmed up out of the southerly forest. 'The camp's next to a creek. It's empty.'

The wiry man spoke swiftly. 'It'd be a long ride. Hiram'll likely come in later. Maybe tomorrow.'

Evan asked if there was food in the camp and the harness-maker nodded. 'Grub, some dirty blankets an' dry kindling.' Frank looked at the wiry man who erupted again with a rush of words. 'I was supposed to get some camp meat. Hiram eats like a damned horse.'

Evan led his horse as did the others but Frank made their captive get astride; if there was shooting he'd be the best target.

There was no shooting. It was a rude, rough camp. What little grass was across the clearing had been just about grazed out of existence.

They used two pairs of chain hobbles

to secure the wiry man to a tree and he protested. According to him the man named Hiram was deadly; a killer who never reasoned beyond a fast draw and a spray of bullets.

What little daylight reached the clearing was fast diminishing. They ate little tinned fish, drank creek water. When the wiry man whined about hunger, they ignored him.

There was little to discuss. As Evan thought, James Bovard and the townsmen he had hired might have located the herd, and then again they might not have. As slowly as cattle moved, Bovard's discovery of his loss hadn't been for several days; cattle being trailed for two or three days would cover considerable ground.

Evan asked the wiry man about the cattle buyer Ordway was to meet. All the prisoner knew was what Tex had said, and that wasn't much. The buyer was a Mexican. He was supposed to have riders with him at the rendezvous. How many the wiry man had no idea.

The buyer and his riders intended to skirt far out and around any ranches on their southerly drive. Hiram, who knew the border country, had told Tex it would require about three weeks to reach the border, and Hiram did not believe the buyer would get down there without encountering soldier patrols.

Hiram had also told Bart when Tex returned to the camp with the money for the cattle, they should kill him and rob his carcass.

Frank Dennis wagged his head as he addressed the captive.

'Fellers like you ever play it straight? Ever keep your word? Mister, I'll tell you what I think: your ma should have strangled you at birth an' raised calves on the milk.'

When nightfall arrived they took turns staying awake. The first one to do this was Evan. He and the prisoner talked until the wiry man collapsed sideways and slept.

The confab left Evan gazing at the cow thief with mixed feelings of contempt and wonder. The prisoner had told of killings as though they were offhand encounters. He had been an outlaw since his sixteenth year.

Wolves howled, a chill arrived and by the time Frank Dennis came over to relieve the lawman, the position of the sinking moon was clear evidence that the new day was not far off, nor was it.

Evan seemed to have hardly closed his eyes when the harness-maker shook him awake. Without an exchange of words they listened to the same sounds of riders. Dawn was breaking but forest gloom lingered and would continue to do so. Frank roused Dougherty, who sat up scratching. He too heard horses, stopped scratching and looked at Evan, who gestured for them to move deeper into the gloom. As he passed the prisoner he said, 'Not a damned word. You understand?' To emphasize his words he pushed a six-gun barrel into the wiry man's middle. Bart nodded his head as he said, 'Ain't supposed to be only Hiram. That's more'n one horse.'

Evan pushed the gun barrel a little. 'Not a sound, you son of a bitch!'

The wiry man nodded again and Evan merged into the dawn gloom among the forest giants behind the prisoner.

The riders were moving slowly, which was normal; they'd been travelling through uphill country. It nevertheless seemed to be an eternity before they were close enough to be discernible passing around big trees.

Evan caught his breath. The lead rider was a lanky, sorrel-headed youth with both hands tied to the saddlehorn. Behind him was James Bovard's niece also with both hands lashed to the horn. Behind her was a less distinct individual and behind him was the fourth rider.

The fourth rider was massively bulky and wore a scraggly beard. He was astride a grey horse built like a log house, square and powerful, the kind of animal his rider required.

Evan let them get to the unkempt camp and dismount like tired people, which they were. Not until the broad, thick man saw the wiry man and called to him did Evan move behind Bart and cock his gun hand. Two other guns were cocked in the gloom, and the burly man stopped in his tracks. His prisoners, wrists tied to saddlehorns could do nothing but hold their breath as Evan addressed the massive, scraggly-bearded man.

'With your left hand, empty the holster!'

The burly man stood as though he had taken root. He made no move to disarm himself. He slowly turned his head but saw nothing, and faced the sound of Evan's voice when he said, 'Who'n hell are you an' what do you want?'

'*Empty the holster!*'

Bart said, 'Do it, Hiram! They're all around. For Chris'sake do it!'

The burly man considered his

prisoners. They were too distant for him to reach as hostages. He used his left hand to drop the six-gun on his right leg. When he'd done that he addressed Bart, 'You double crossin' son of a bitch!' and Bart moved his legs to make the chain hobbles rattle. 'Never had a chance,' he said.

Evan moved close to the wiry man, close enough to ram his gunbarrel into the prisoner's back over the kidneys. Bart flinched and made a little squawk of pain.

Frank Dennis, also a solidly built individual came out of the dawn gloom, half spun the burly man and said, 'Face down with your hands over your head. *Do it!*'

The burly man obeyed, but ponderously and when he craned around the harness-maker shoved a cocked six-gun in his face. The burly man got belly-down and pushed his hands ahead.

Dougherty approached the prisoners with his big clasp knife, cut them loose and did not reply when the girl asked who he was.

Frank said, 'Evan, their horses is in poor shape.'

The marshal could see that. 'Hobble them out in the clearing.'

As Frank moved toward the animals the man face-down spoke. 'What do you bastards want?' Frank spoke before the lawman could. 'Hang you'n weasel-face over yonder.'

As Frank got busy caring for the animals Evan put up his six-gun, walked down where the burly man was lying and knelt. 'How'd you catch 'em?' He did not have to say who he meant. The burly man raised his head and faced the marshal. 'On a back trail, in plain sight like greenhorns.'

'An' what did you figure to do with 'em?'

'Tex said for me to take 'em back up here. He said we could hang the boys but keep the girl until he got back.'

The lanky youth, rubbing his wrists spoke for the first time. 'We made good time. Too good, I expect. That man was waitin' in some brush. When he come up there he was holdin' his horse with a cocked gun. His name's . . . '

Evan interrupted. 'I know his name. How far ahead was the cattle?'

'Maybe a day or such a matter.'

'Did you see any sign of James Bovard with some riders?'

'No. Didn't see another human bein' until that one come out in front of us with a cocked pistol.'

Evan faced the girl and she smiled. 'A knight in shining armour,' she said, and at the blank look she got from the marshal she also said, 'It's in a book I read. The knight in shining armour comes riding up when . . . '

'Ma'am,' Evan interrupted; 'who's takin' care of Bovard's boy?'

'An old midwife from Rock City. Her'n the doctor. It bothered my uncle leavin' Clint but the doctor said Clint'd be in good hands.' She cocked her head a little. 'I was never so glad to see someone in my life, Marshal.'

The other boy, smaller and tired-looking repeated that, phrasing it differently but his sincerity was equal. He also said, 'Hiram knocked me down. Mind if I go over and hit him back?'

Evan didn't mind but the lad didn't hit the burly man, he kicked him hard in the side, went back beside his horse and smiled.

Frank returned from the little clearing to ask Evan what he intended to do with Hiram, and got a short reply. 'Take him back'n lock him up, or hang him, there's lots of trees around.'

Frank was looking down when he said, 'Hang him.'

The wiry man broke a long silence. 'You'll lose a fortune. He knows where there's caches. For all we partnered, he never told me where the loot from banks'n trains and stages is hid.'

Dougherty was looking downward when he put in his two-bits worth. 'He'd lie. Hang the son of a bitch an' we can head for home.'

This is what they did, but it wasn't

a simple matter of using Hiram's big horse to hoist him, he put up one hell of a fight. For a time he seemed to be making headway against the odds, but when Evan put his weight behind a low blow and Hiram doubled over in pain, the fight was over.

As they boosted Hiram to his horse, hands tied in back, he looked over their heads and cursed a blue streak in the wiry man's direction. It rolled off the other prisoner like water off a duck's back. In fact, as Mike Dougherty got the nod from Evan to lead the big horse ahead, and Hiram lost the stirrups while making gagging sounds, the wiry man watched and smiled, even after Hiram stopped contorting.

6

Tired Men and Horses

They left the rugged highlands and regardless of the perilous footing were in pleasant shade, but when it was possible to see the open country they encountered heat.

Because Evan took a direct southerly route instead of returning to the road their attention concentrated on safe footing, avoiding impassable places and for most of the way riding in single file, which were the reasons there was little conversation.

There were other reasons, such as leaving Hiram six feet off the ground back yonder, and Evan's disillusionment about being unable to continue westerly to find Bovard. He was resigned; whatever happened elsewhere, the hand fate had dealt him precluded a major part in other things.

When they left the uplands, came out of the canyon where the river ran, Lee Bovard eased up beside the marshal and said, 'We owe you, Mister Stannard.'

He smiled thinly at the handsome woman. 'Just luck, ma'am.'

'If you hadn't been waiting at their camp . . . '

He changed the subject. 'If you ever do something like that again, remember, outlaws got as much interest in their back trail as they have getting clear.'

She accepted what was a mild rebuke without comment.

When the roar of the river was behind them, Evan angled in the direction of Rock City. A mile farther along the woman said she would like to split off, head for home and care for her wounded relative.

Evan was agreeable but he had a question. 'If you're James Bovard's niece, that means he had a sister or a brother, don't it?'

Her expression turned gently pensive. 'He had no sister or brother. You knew that, didn't you?'

'No ma'am. I only know what I've heard an' that sort of information is most likely wrong.'

'I was found under a big basket after Mexican raiders from below the line raided a village, killed everyone and drove the livestock south when it was over.'

'You're not related?'

'He raised me with the help of several women at the posts where he was sent while he was in the army.'

Evan considered the handsome woman. 'Did a good job, I'd say.'

Her smile returned. 'One of the women was Navajo. She'd take me far off and we'd play a game of tracking. First mice and rats, then snakes and coyotes. She could read sign where there wasn't any. Her name was Sheila Begay. Her clan was very large. She wasn't accepted by some because her father had been a white soldier. She needed someone to love and so did I.'

The handsome woman raised her gaze to include miles of empty land. 'Sheila died when I was sixteen. I didn't think she was old enough to die, but she was.'

The dark eyes swung to Evan. 'Mister Bovard was like a father to me, and to the boys who came here with him. Clint's mother disappeared. I heard years later that she ran off with a trader who wore a big diamond stick pin and drove a buggy that had tassels around the top. We never talked about her.'

'Clint was her son?'

'Yes. All this was a long time ago. After Clint's dad was discharged . . . '

'What about the redheaded lad and the shorter one?'

'They were abandoned. He found them in a place called Tanque Verde, a railroad town where they were being forced to fight other boys. The men made bets. He brought them to me to patch up . . . He's been our father. I think I know what folks think of James Bovard, the man who killed his own father.'

'That's what he did, ma'am.'

'My name is Lee not ma'am. He had good reason.'

She ended the conversation there by standing in her stirrups before saying, 'Goodbye, Mister Stannard.'

He called after her. 'My name's Evan.'

She must have heard because she twisted in the saddle and waved.

Dougherty came forward to ask where the girl was going. When the marshal explained, he did it while watching her grow to ant size under the dazzling sun.

Dougherty had another question. 'You didn't want to hang that scrawny one back yonder too?'

Evan turned his face, the girl was no longer in sight. 'I need a lot of answers, Mike.'

'Seems to me he give 'em already.'

Evan thinly smiled. 'We can still hang him. Let's pick up the gait so's we can reach town before dark.'

That is what they did, alternately loping and walking until they had rooftops in sight, then they slackened to a steady walk.

Evan veered to the coach road and entered Rock City from the north. There were very few people abroad for an excellent reason, it was suppertime.

Mark Wheeler saw them pass; he had emerged from the eatery and was sucking his teeth which he stopped doing. The horsemen did not look in his direction. He saw the dark, wiry man with hands tied in back. He hastened to the livery barn where his youthful hostler was dunging out and arrived there as the lawman swung down and held out his reins. Wheeler took them while looking at the tuckered-up horses Dougherty and Frank Dennis were climbing off. He made a little clucking sound but offered no remonstrate. The horses had been used hard. The men who were responsible did not seem likely to take even a mild scolding. Wheeler was intrigued by the boys and the 'breed-looking sinewy man who was yanked from the saddle and whose hands were tied in back.

Evan, Frank and Mike herded the others up to the jailhouse. Up there, after firing up a hanging lantern, the marshal told the Bovard lads to tell the rooming-house man he had sent them, to give them a room and show them where the wash-house was out back. In the morning they could head for home.

After the lads left, the marshal perched on the edge of his desk eyeing the man calling himself Bart Smith. Dougherty mumbled something about opening the saloon and left. Frank Dennis took the chair along the front wall and sat slightly sideways. Although he was as hungry as a bitch wolf he had no intention of leaving the jailhouse just yet.

Evan asked Smith where he had

joined up with Bovard's fired range boss and got a cryptic reply. 'At Porterville, up north. Hiram'n me got to talkin' with Tex an' when he offered rider's pay if we'd come down here an' help him settle some old scores, we took him up on it.'

'Did Tex mention rustling Bovard cattle?'

'Yep. The way he said it he knew the country real well, an' knew where to cut off a sizeable bunch without no one knowin' about it until maybe next fall when the gather was made.' Smith bobbed his head like a bird. 'It was the truth. Them cattle was about as far from the Bovard yard an' the other range as cattle could be. It went good, except for a few damned cut-backs.'

Frank Dennis had a question. 'When Hiram'n you figured to kill Ordway after he come back with the money, you figured to go back up north?'

Smith eyed the harness-maker. 'Go south, mister. All the way to Messico. Hiram said him'n me was gettin' too well known to stay up here. I figured he was right.'

'You ever been to Messico?'

'No, but Hiram's been down there. He said with money we could live like kings.'

Dennis, who had bought hides in Mexico over the years rolled his eyes. 'Mister, if you went down there with money you'd wake up with your throat cut. They're not only poor as snakes, they're treacherous. I know for a fact they've killed travellers down there for their boots.' Frank glared at Evan. 'Maybe you'd ought to let this son of a bitch ride south.'

Evan went to the wall behind his desk, took down the big copper ring with one key on it and jerked his head for the wiry man to precede him. After locking the prisoner in a strap steel cage the marshal straightened up as he said, 'Gnaw your way out,' started away as Bart Smith said, 'I know where one of them caches is. I can draw you a map.'

Evan said, 'Sure you can,' returned to the office, flung the keyring on his desk and looked at the harness-maker. 'You hungry?'

Frank arose. 'I could chew myself through a rattlesnake beginnin' at the tail if someone would hold its head.'

The caféman was scrubbing his counter when his customers walked in. He raised his eyes without smiling. 'I'm fixin' to close up,' he said, and continued swabbing the counter.

Frank Dennis sat down. 'We missed three, four feedings, friend.'

He and the caféman exchanged a long stare before the caféman tucked the wiping rag under his apron and said, 'All's I got is antelope steak, yestiddy's spuds an' cold coffee.'

The harness-maker smiled expansively. 'Exactly what we was goin' to order. Heat up the coffee.'

Evan sat, rocked far back and closed his eyes. Frank said, 'You wore out? I am too an' my butt is sore.'

The caféman banged pans on the

118

stove. They ignored this demonstration of surliness. Frank asked about the prisoner. Evan leaned on the counter when he replied. 'Call a town meetin' to try him, an' hang the son of a bitch.'

When their platters arrived the food had been purposefully and randomly piled. Evan went to work eating but the harness-maker looked from the mess in front of him to the beetle-browed caféman. 'Henry,' he said quietly. 'Today we hung a man. You want to clean this plate or get your gawddamned throat cut?'

Evan was too famished to heed any of this but when he picked up the cup of joe, it was cold. He held the cup out. 'Hot, or I'll slit your pouch an' pull your leg through it.'

Outside, the night was cool and star-speckled. The lawman and Frank Dennis parted. Dougherty's saloon was brightly lit. Someone with two right hands was playing 'Oh Susanna' on Mike's piano, which had survived the overland trip in a conestoga and hadn't been touched since.

Marshal Stannard thought of the girl. Her youthful companions too, but mostly the girl. It did not seem that he had been asleep more than a few minutes although the sun was halfway above the easterly world when someone pounded on his door. 'Marshal! Git up! Marshal! You hear me? Git up!'

Evan sat up, rubbed his eyes and when whoever was in the hall hit the door again he called to them to get away from the door, arose, yanked on his britches, got into his shirt and opened the door. The nervous nellie who was corralyard boss for the stage company was out there standing stiff as a ramrod. Evan reached inside his shirt to scratch. 'What the hell's wrong now?' he asked, and got a shrill rapidfire reply.

'That Bovard feller's down at Wheeler's barn. He's been hurt. He's got two prisoners. A dead Messican tied across a horse an' another one that no one can understand. Bovard's left arm is in a sling. He's a bloody mess. You got to hurry!'

Evan considered the corralyard boss. 'Go tell Wheeler to fetch the preacher. Tell him to bring his doctor's satchel down to the livery barn.'

'Are you comin'?'

'For Chris' sake, you mind if I get my boots on?' Evan slammed the door. Later, fully dressed and wearing his shell belt with its holstered Colt he left the room and nearly collided with the rooming-house owner still in his nightdress and tasselled cap. Before the older man could speak Evan gave him a gentle push and walked to the roadway door, passed beyond it while the rooming-house owner went grumblingly in the direction of his living-quarters.

The corralyard boss was right; when Evan entered the livery barn runway with a red rising sun at his back, the liveryman was standing on a bench turning up the wick of his runway lantern, and three men sagged on a wall bench while another was face down. The liveryman shot Evan a look and began caring for the horses. He did not reappear until his runway was nearly empty. He stared at the big corpse.

James Bovard looked up at the lawman. 'Is there a doctor in Rock City?'

'No, but the Methodist preacher's been actin' as one. He'll be along.'

Evan gazed at the corpse in its embroidered leather *vaquero* short jacket and britches. Bovard also looked at the dead man as he said, 'I knew I couldn't catch 'em where they was waitin' for the cattle, so we rode due west an' waited. The drive was noisy, riders yellin' in Spanish. Daylight was fading when we saw 'em comin' an' set up a bushwhack on both sides of their trail . . . Mister Stannard I'll tell you one thing for a fact, those Messicans fought like tigers.'

'The cattle, Mister Bovard?'

'They stampeded easterly. By tomorrow they'll be back home.' Bovard jutted his jaw in the direction of the dead *vaquero*. 'That's the head In'ian. Accordin' to the one we got alive his name's Sixto Fernandez an' he's a big rancher down in Messico. I got no idea which of us hit him, but he was bellowin' like a bull an' led the charge in my direction. I got no idea who hit me in the arm but I saw Fernandez go off his horse. When it was over an' we had one that got set afoot, he identified Fernandez . . . Marshal?'

'Frank Dennis, Mike Dougherty an' I stumbled on to their camp in the uplands, hung one and brought one back with us. The one we hung had your niece and the boys. I sent 'em home.'

Evan eyed the captured Mexican, a thin, dark, undersized man wearing huge Chihuahua spurs who would not raise his face. The men who had ridden with Bovard left, one at a time, wore down, too numb to talk.

The corralyard boss arrived with the minister, a tousle-headed beanstalk of a man carrying a small black satchel who did not await either an introduction nor explanation but went to work on Bovard's injured arm. The liveryman produced a bottle of rye whiskey from his harness room. Only the preacher declined. The liveryman drank the most before disappearing back into his harness room to cache the bottle. When he returned he dragged the chair over, climbed up and blew down the mantle of his runway light. The sun was high and climbing, Rock City was bright from one end to the other and inevitably the townsmen who had ridden with James Bovard had told their tale before bedding down.

The minister sent Evan over to the mercantile for proper bandaging and during his absence the minister straightened up looking directly at James Bovard who misinterpreted the look and rummaged with his right hand for pocket money.

The shockle-head scarecrow with his collar on backwards ignored the hand with money and said, 'From what I've heard, Mister Bovard, you've broke the Lord's commandments. I don't want your money, I want to redeem your soul. For splintin' that arm I require a penance.'

The swarthy man was staring up at the preacher.

'Every Sunday for one year, Mister Bovard, you come to church. You'n yours, and you'n I'll pray privately for the redemption of your soul.'

Bovard said nothing, watched the minister take bandaging material from the marshal, remained silent until the bandaging was completed and watched the preacher leave. Finally he looked at the lawman. 'You know what he said? For me to come to church every damned Sunday for a year.'

Evan nodded. 'That's what he does every time he patches someone up. Mister Bovard . . . ?'

The swarthy man gingerly moved his

arm; the pain was negligible. He looked at Evan again. 'Every blessed Sunday for a solid year?'

Evan ignored the question. 'I got a place at the rooming-house if you'd like to bed down for a day or two.'

'You said Lee an' the boys is all right?'

'I said I sent 'em home. I expect they're all right. Mister Bovard you didn't happen to run across Tex Ordway did you?'

'No. Just the Messicans drivin' cattle south.'

'Tex is behind everythin', the cattle theft, the shootin' of your boy. I got a prisoner at the jailhouse you should talk to, after you've rested up.'

Bovard arose, looked for Wheeler the liveryman, did not see him so called his name. Wheeler emerged from his harness room unctuously smiling. He missed the low step from the harness room to the earthen runway and sprawled half atop the dead Mexican. When he raised up he made a bleating

126

squawk and scrambled unsteadily to his feet.

Bovard and the marshal exchanged a look. Evan said, 'I'll get your horse.' During his absence the liveryman considered the nondescript Mexican prisoner who had not made a sound since being pulled off a horse and pushed down on a stool. 'Hey, *paisano*,' he said. 'They goin' to hang you,' and gripped his own throat as he made strangling sounds. The Mexican watched and stoically shrugged. He was as wiry and spare as the man who said his name was Bart Smith, and only a few shades darker. He was also about the same age if looks meant anything and about half the loops in his crossed bandoleers were empty, as was his hip-holster. He held out one hand and said, 'Wheesky, *señor*.'

Wheeler's little pale eyes did not waver when he replied. 'Not on your stinkin' damned life,' and went unsteadily back into his harness room. The *bandolero* looked at James

Bovard and said, '*Gachupín?*'

The swarthy man's reply was curt. '*Indio.*'

Nothing more was said until Evan brought up Bovard's animal and held out the braided rawhide reins. Bovard arose, staggered and sat back down.

Evan led the horse away to be off-saddled. When he returned there were people across the road staring down into the sun-bright runway.

Evan held out a hand, steadied the swarthy man and jerked his head for the Mexican to walk ahead to the door-less wide front opening.

If the Mexican thought of making a run for it he had to abandon the idea. The opposite roadway where sunlight had not reached was lined with people watching, the men silent and as expressionless as stones, every one of them armed.

They got as far as the jailhouse where Evan flung open the door for the Mexican to enter first, then waited for James Bovard to do the same. Bovard went to a bench and eased down, raised his legs, carefully lowered his bandaged arm and closed his eyes.

Evan locked the Mexican in his only unoccupied cage, returned to the office and waited until Frank Dennis walked in to take the chair against the front wall before saying someone ought to ride to Three Bells and tell them out there James Bovard was back and had a wounded arm.

The saddle-maker looked Evan straight in the eyes. 'Someone else, Frank. My butt's tender as a spanked baby's bottom.' Dennis saw the filthy, bandaged man on the bench, sighed and rolled his eyes. 'I'll do it. When he wakes up from sleepin' on that bench he's goin' to be sore in places he didn't even know he had.'

7

The Lawman's Idea

Frank was right. James Bovard did not awaken until there were long shadows. He made three attempts to sit up before he accomplished it.

Across at the desk watching, the marshal arose and took his private bottle of pop-skull to the man on the bench, who eyed it briefly, then took it and swallowed twice before handing back the bottle.

When Bovard spoke the sound was not unlike someone drawing a wood saw over a piece of steel. 'How long I been out?'

'Since this morning. I'll fetch you somethin' to eat.'

'I feel like a herd of horses run over me and the last one . . . '

'The harness-maker's gone out yonder

to let 'em know you're back.'

Bovard shifted gingerly and groaned. Evan said, 'I thought In'ians was real stoic.'

'You just heard the other half. You got any water?'

Evan brought the olla and Bovard drank deeply, ran his uninjured hand across his mouth and groaned again. 'They better bring a wagon,' he said, and fixed both dark eyes on the marshal. 'You got Ordway?'

'No. All I got is your Messican an' Ordway's runnin' mate.'

Bovard leaned as though to arise at the exact moment the preacher walked in carrying his little satchel. As before he offered no greeting, nor more than very briefly glanced at the lawman. He approached Bovard, paused and wrinkled his nose. 'Whiskey's the Devil's brew, Mister Bovard.'

The swarthy man looked up. 'Him'n me got somethin' in common, Reverend. What're you goin' to do?'

'See if there's inflammation or

infection. Hold still.'

Evan went to stand by the little barred front wall window, ignored the sounds over where James Bovard sat as the preacher worked on him.

Where was Tex Ordway? In retrospect he saw the mistake he had made. Ordway was supposed to return to the camp where Hiram and his scrawny partner would be waiting.

Now, when Ordway rode up there and saw Hiram hanging from a tree and no sign of the wiry man, unless Ordway was a fool he would certainly figure out something had gone wrong; whether he was a good enough sign reader to figure out three horsemen had been at the camp, or whether he thought the wiry man had killed Hiram, the result would be the same; Ordway would leave. With the money from the rustled Three Bells' cattle he would be able to go a long distance.

For Evan Stannard the question was simply — which way would Ordway go? If he could determine that and providing it didn't rain . . . He looked over where Bovard was as rigid as a rock, looked back out into the sunsmash, and had a thought he knew James Bovard for one, and probably others as well, would not like.

Lee Bovard could read sign like an Indian. Better than most Indians.

His attention was jerked back toward the far wall where the preacher was talking. It was his habit to dwell on some words and to articulate others very clearly.

''There is only sin that comes from killing people'. It says in the Good Book 'those that wield the sword shall perish by the sword. Let this man go; somewhere down his road he will be smitten'. It is God's word, and anyway, you won't be able to sit a horse for a long time. Do you understand this omen? In His wisdom it is decreed that you not find this Ordway. 'Vengeance is mine, saith the Lord'. Be satisfied punishment will come upon Ordway.' The preacher paused. 'There's no infection, for which you should get on your knees and give thanks, as filthy as your clothes are.' The minister was closing his little satchel when he also said, 'The road to Hell is blazed by those seeking salvation. I'll see you again in a few days, meanwhile don't use that arm, don't even move it. You're not a young man; the healing will take time. And remember my fee, Mister Bovard, every Sunday for a year.'

After the minister departed James Bovard put a sour look on the marshal. Before he could speak Evan smiled as he said, 'Snow gets pretty deep in the winter. You'll need a big stout team to get you to town some Sundays.'

Bovard did not smile. He eased forward to stand up. Evan watched and wagged his head. 'Set. I'll fetch somethin' to eat. Mister Bovard, I mean it. Set *down*!'

James Bovard eased down and leaned to see past the open door as the lawman hiked in the direction of the eatery. He stood up again, took two steps, reached with his right hand to grip the desk's edge, waited a moment then returned to the bench. Someone in the cell room was bellowing about being hungry. Bovard yelled back using angry profanity. There was not another sound from the cell room.

It was close to midday when all but Bovard's niece arrived out front with a light dray wagon whose bed was full of hay and blankets. Bovard knew who it was when someone said, 'Let down the tailgate. If Lee'd come she could have set with him on the way back.'

Bovard arose, too swiftly, his heart pounded and his vision blurred. He sat down again and swore for a solid sixty seconds without repeating himself.

Evan was returning from the café when he saw the two youths and the wagon. They saw him too and waited until he was close before explaining their purpose. Evan jerked his head for them to follow and led the way inside where James Bovard held out his good hand for the platter of food.

The boys showed their awkwardness when they told Bovard he looked good, and got a sour glance from the eating man. Evan told the boys what the preacher had said. They nodded and watched Bovard lick the last vestiges of food from the platter, put it aside and lean to arise. Evan said, 'Easy,' and the tall redheaded boy moved close to help. Bovard shook his head at the boy. Evan crossed to the bench and took the injured man by his good arm. He helped the swarthy man down the steps to the plankwalk and over to the lowered tailgate. The boys helped with the lifting. Bovard locked his jaws. When they told him to lie back atop the blankets he surprised Evan by obeying without even a scowl.

As the boys climbed up, James Bovard turned dark eyes toward the marshal. 'Stay out of it, Mister Stannard. He's mine.'

Evan neither spoke nor nodded. He stepped back as the shortest youth talked up the stud-necked big mare between the shafts.

People watched from both sides of the road. The boys ignored them as they left town to the north and bounced over the westerly berm where they left the road heading westerly toward home.

Frank Dennis arrived in town. When he passed the wagon he waved. The boys waved back. Frank left his animal at Wheeler's barn, walked up to the jailhouse and sat sideways on the chair against the front wall. Evan got him a cup of coffee and waited until the harness-maker had half emptied it before speaking.

'That doctor out there'll wait until Bovard gets there. He told me he had to get back to his private practice.'

'How's Clint doin'?'

Frank held out the cup to be refilled and did not speak again until he got the cup back. 'The doctor says, young or not, he'll be maybe a year before he can set a horse. He said, by rights the boy should have died. He said a person can only lose so much blood then nothing short of Gawd himself can keep 'em alive.'

'How's Lee?'

Frank's eyebrows climbed. 'Lee?'

'The girl, Frank. Lee Bovard.'

Dennis put the cup aside and gingerly shifted position. 'She took over from the midwife.' Frank paused glancing at the racked-up guns on the far wall. 'Did you know she's not Bovard's real kin?'

'Yes. She told me. An' those boys too.'

The harness-maker had just seen a revelation — he'd ridden all the way back to Rock City figuring to drop on the marshal and enjoy the look of shock — wither. He arose. 'I think killin' the old man with everyone watchin' sort of set folks' minds about James Bovard.'

The marshal agreed. 'They pegged him a gun-fighter.'

'When they set the decent things he's done against that killin' . . . '

'It'll take time, Frank.'

'I expect so. How bad off is he?'

'Accordin' to the preacher he'll be months healing, but he'll make it.'

The harness-maker considered the gun rack again. 'You think he'll twiddle his thumbs for that long?' Frank Dennis brought his gaze back to the marshal. 'His niece, or whatever she is, asked about you.'

They looked at each other for over a period of silence then the harness-maker said, 'I got to get back to work,' and left.

The marshal sat loose for a long time before arising to take a booted Winchester and head for the livery barn. Down there he gave Mark Wheeler a crumpled greenback. Wheeler's brows drew together. 'What's that for?'

'For you feedin' the prisoners until I get back. Don't let 'em out. Don't even unlock their cages, slide food under the doors.'

Wheeler continued to frown at the money in his hand. 'For how long?'

'I don't know. Maybe a few days,

maybe longer.' Stannard went for his horse. When he led it up to be cross-tied during the process of rigging it out the liveryman, faintly frowning, watched in dogged silence. He had pocketed the greenback. As the marshal led the horse out back before mounting Wheeler said, 'You mind tellin' me where you're goin'?'

Evan smiled. 'Remember, don't unlock their cages,' and nudged the horse, leaving the liveryman standing in the alley watching as the lawman rode northward until he found a wide, overgrown place between two buildings, turned west and kept riding.

Wheeler returned to his harness room, sat down and wagged his head. He wouldn't unlock the cages no matter what. He was truthful with himself to the point where he spoke aloud. 'I don't like it.'

Evan did not hasten, his saddle-bags were full, his bedroll was snug behind the cantle and there were larks in the grass and somewhere far ahead a mammy cow bawled for her baby who, like all babies with a stomach full of milk continued to lie in shade and ignore its mother's calling.

When he came up atop the north-south landswell easterly of the Three Bells' yard, he stopped. There was no one in sight but out back of the barn there was dust. He eased down, passed between the barn and walked down through. The two boys had roped a big stud colt. It was dragging them around the corral as though they were weightless. Evan climbed between the poles and when the lads came abreast grimly hanging on to the rope, he called to them.

'Drop it!'

They hadn't seen him climb into the corral. They ignored his words as they flashed past, heels dug in raising dust. He waited until the stud colt was coming back, moved in front and flagged with his hat. The colt was startled and jammed to a halt. Evan yelled to the boys to give slack, which they did so that when the horse jumped out the lariat flapped around him. Evan moved to block the colt again and this time when the animal halted slack in the rope allowed the loop to sag down on its shoulders.

Evan interrupted the colt three more times before the lariat fell off. He recovered it, shook out a loop and allowed the colt to flash past him twice. The third time he made a backhand overhead throw, caught the colt's front feet, took up the slack and when the horse tried to lunge it fell. Evan called to the boys, 'Hold his head on the ground an' the two of you set on his neck.'

Because a horse cannot recover from a fall unless he can throw his head up, the boys not only sat on his neck, they straddled it. The redheaded one gripped both nostrils and held on for dear life.

The horse struggled, discovered it could not arise and stopped fighting.

Evan walked over to ask why they'd

roped the big colt. The answer he got kept him silent. The smallest boy said, 'We're goin' to break him to ride.'

Evan said nothing. Horse-breakers were not born, they were made, and those two were going to begin their education the moment they got a saddle and bridle on that big stout stud colt.

He left them, crossed the yard and was approaching the porch when a grizzled stranger emerged. He said, 'I'm Doctor Phipps from Montross. If you came to see Mister Bovard I got him sedated an' he won't come out of it until after suppertime.'

Evan gave his name, hesitated a moment then asked if Lee Bovard was around. The grizzled man did not answer, he jerked his head.

Inside, the house smelled powerfully of disinfectant. The window coverings had been drawn, the parlour was not only dark it was also cool.

Doctor Phipps hesitated. 'You can talk to the lad, Marshal. The young lady's in there with him.'

When Evan appeared in the bedroom doorway the lad in the bed and the girl both looked up. It was dark in the room. Evan dropped his hat on a littered small table and smiled in the direction of the bed. 'You look good,' he said, which he could not actually see from the doorway but it was what folks were supposed to tell injured people.

Lee Bovard cleared a chair and put it next to the bed. She then would have left the room if the lawman hadn't continued to block the door. He said, 'I'd like to talk to you directly.'

She said she'd be in the parlour and he stepped aside for her to pass.

Clint Bovard dryly said, 'I told Pa I ain't sure the Rock River country is good for our health.'

Evan eased down on the chair. 'Did you know the feller who bushwhacked you is dead?'

'Did you find him?'

'I leaned on the rope. He's up yonder some miles hangin' from a tree. His name was Hiram. If he had a last name

144

I never heard it. How do you feel?'

'Like a band of hostiles run over me an' the last one drug his feet. Did you meet the doctor?'

Evan nodded. 'You know your pa got hurt?'

'Yes. We talked a little after they brought him back.'

'Accordin' to the preacher in town who patched him up it'll be next spring before he can straddle a horse.'

The lad's dark eyes did not leave the lawman's face. 'He's not goin' to be happy about that.'

Evan shrugged. 'That's not goin' to matter, boy. If he can't, why then he can't. I'd like a few words with him.'

'The medicine man wants him to sleep round the clock. He rebandaged the wound. He said Pa lost a sight of blood an' that it takes folks a long time to make more.'

Evan leaned to arise when Clinton Bovard spoke again without taking his eyes off the lawman. 'Lee told me how you'n your friends ambushed them renegades, that you caught 'em both flat-footed . . . Did you hang the other one?'

'No. Got him locked up in town. He told us about all we wanted to know.'

Evan arose. 'If I can't talk to your pa I'd like to talk to Lee.'

Clint said, 'Come back any time, Mister Stannard.'

From the doorway Evan paused to smile. The lad in the bed was not the same lad Evan had encountered in Dougherty's saloon a while back.

Lee Bovard was waiting. She'd drawn off two cups of coffee, one she held in both hands, the other cup was on a little marble-topped table near a leather chair. She nodded and Evan sat in the leather chair. She regarded him steadily from dark eyes.

It was up to him to open the conversation which he made no attempt to do as long as they looked steadily at one another, so he leaned forward regarding the floor when he spoke.

'Ordway's loose. One way or another we took care of the others, but Tex is gone.'

She put the cup aside before speaking. 'And you need someone who can pick up his sign and track him.'

The marshal continued to stare at the floor. On the ride out he rehearsed different ways he could approach her to ride with him on a trail that might involve being away for some time, and had not come up with anything.

She interrupted his reverie. 'Marshal? Is that it?'

His eyes came up slowly. 'Yes'm, that's it. I can show you where their camp was. He was supposed to head back there. If you could pick up his sign from there . . . '

'Do you have any idea how long this might take?' she asked.

He answered candidly that he had no idea where the trail might take them and she seemed to understand. 'There

147

has to be someone to take care of Clint and Jim.'

'The doctor?'

'He says he's done all he can do for the present. He said he'd come back in a few weeks.'

'The boys?'

Her smile was fleeting. 'The midwife from town? She's good with 'em.'

He eased back in the chair. She asked if he'd like more coffee. He didn't. 'Mister Bovard . . .'

'I'll talk to him. He won't like it but . . .'

'He told me in town not to hunt for Ordway. He wanted to take care of that himself.'

Again the fleeting smile appeared. 'The doctor told him he'd be unable to ride for several months. By then the trail will be cold, won't it?' As she arose she asked a question, 'When, Marshal?'

'I'd like to strike out early tomorrow.'

'Will you ask the midwife to come out and stay until we return?'

He also arose. It hadn't been at all difficult. He would speculate about that later. She'd held the initiative almost from the start. He went after his hat. Clint was sleeping. When he returned to the parlour she was waiting. 'I'll meet you in town about sunrise tomorrow,' she told him, and took him to the door where dust was rising from behind the barn. She asked what the boys were doing, he told her and she sighed but said nothing. He dropped his hat on, went to the steps and turned. 'I wish there was some other way. This isn't goin' to be easy, ma'am.'

'I thought we understood that my name was Lee, not ma'am.'

He nodded without smiling. 'Lee . . . how'll you handle Mister Bovard?'

'I won't have to. Doctor Phipps puts him to sleep as soon as the pain starts. Marshal . . . ?'

It was his turn and he took it. 'Evan, just plain Evan.'

The fleeting smile came and went. 'Evan, if we find him I'd like to fetch him back alive. Jim would like that.'

Evan started down the steps as he said, 'If it's possible, Lee, but from what I know of Ordway . . . See you in the morning.'

8

The Trail

He was busy an hour or so before sunrise the following morning. He packed an extra set of saddle-bags and when the sun arrived and she rode toward the jailhouse from the north roadway, he was sure he had forgotten something.

She tied up out front and appeared in the doorway, smiling. She was bundled inside a horseman's coat with the sheep pelt on the inside. She was also wearing a shell belt and holstered Colt. He asked if she'd had breakfast and was relieved when she nodded because the cranky caféman would not be ready for business for another hour.

While she waited he went down to look in on his prisoners. He was bundled for riding, which was obvious.

151

The Mexican said nothing but the wiry man did. 'You goin' to be gone long?' he asked and the marshal ignored the question to say, 'You'll be taken care of; fed and watered. I'll come back as soon as I can.'

The wiry man grinned. 'You're goin' to need wings to find him, Marshal.'

'Find who?'

'Tex Ordway. He knows them mountains like an In'ian, an' maybe he won't stop there.'

'Where would he go?' Evan asked and got a malicious smile from the wiry man. 'If I knew why would I tell you?'

'Because if you don't I'll come in there an' work on you until you can't stand without help.'

The prisoner, who did not care much for the mean-tempered former Three Bells' range boss, considered Evan through the steel of his cell. Bart Smith had a mean streak. He was also a malicious individual. When he spoke that false grin was back in place.

'If he ain't in the rough country he's got reason to be in the Cloverdale country. You know where that is?'

Evan nodded. 'Why would he go there?'

'He lived over there for six, seven years. He knows folks. But just as likely he'd ride south, toward Messico. A man can lose hisself down there real easy, an' if he's got money he can hire Messicans to watch out for him.'

Evan turned to face the dark prisoner. Their glances caught and held. Behind him Bart, Smith said, 'Take your pick, Marshal, north or south.'

Evan left the cell room, helped Lee tie the extra pair of saddle-bags in place, swung astride and led off northward out of town. Among those who saw him leave were Mike Dougherty and the disagreeable caféman, otherwise if folks were stirring they were more concerned with breakfast than riders.

There was a chill that would linger, the sky was clear and visibility was excellent. As they rode he considered

153

the odds; they were two to one that Ordway had gone north.

He told Lee what Smith had said and she agreed they should go north. She was astride a short-backed buckskin built like a brick house. When Lee saw him assessing her animal she said, 'He's tough as a boiled owl,' and Evan nodded; buckskins were noted for toughness. If this one had a drawback it was that he was short-backed; short-backed horses loped and ran without much flexibility. Lee said, 'My uncle said to take him.'

'What else did he say?'

Her fleeting smile came and went. 'He said I shouldn't go with you, that you could hire a tracker. He didn't get mad . . . He was drowsy from medicine.'

'How about the boys?'

'They were asleep when I left.'

'They wouldn't try an' follow?'

'No, not one of them can read sign.' Lee looked far ahead where the forbidding, dark uplands blocked out other northward country. In anticipation of her thoughts Evan said, 'We'll try the camp first; then a wide place in the road called Cloverdale. It's about sixty miles upcountry. Ordway used to live there, a prisoner back at the jailhouse told me that.'

They remained on the road until the sun was high then left the road in the same place Evan, Dougherty and Frank Dennis had left it before. Here, Lee did not lift her gaze until Evan drew rein where the encounter with the wiry man had taken place. She jutted her jaw, 'South,' she said. Evan led off again.

Before they came out of the timber he told her she might want to hang back a spell. 'We hanged a feller up ahead. I'll go cut him down.'

She edged around him and kept on riding. When they reached the clearing she was not shocked but the marshal was. There was no sign of Hiram nor the rope which had been used to hang him.

Lee sashayed her horse slowly while

155

Evan went to the hang tree. On one of Lee's sashays she stopped beside Evan and pointed to a faint smudge. 'Indian,' she said.

He accepted that. If hide-out tomahawks had found the body, had taken it down to appropriate whatever had been in Hiram's pockets as well as the rope, what had they done with the carcass?

Evan's speculation was cut short. Lee was at the edge of the little grazed clearing when she called to him. 'If you an' your friends rode toward Rock City, an' if the only other person riding a shod horse was here, there are his tracks.'

Evan had to lean. Even then although he could see crushed grazed-over grass stubble he could not make out the sign well enough to know it had been made by a shod horse.

Lee moved away on a slack rein until she eventually dismounted and moved away from her animal. Evan also dismounted but he stood with his horse watching the woman. The upland silence was deafening, nor did it make the lawman feel easy knowing what he'd never known nor heard of before: there were hide-outs in the wild uplands.

It was not actually a surprise. He'd heard stories of the army's inability to thoroughly search the wild highlands. It was not uncommon for hide-outs to live in secret places like hunted animals, always on guard, always watching, rarely seen and even more rarely making raids.

Lee beckoned to him from an uppermost edge of the little clearing. When he led his horse over to her she held out her right hand. She had found two strips of smoke-tanned leather, the kind Indians commonly wore on the heels of their moccasins to drag over and cover their tracks. She smiled. 'The idea's all right. It just don't help much. It's as easy to follow the drag marks as the footprints.' She put the strips in a shirt pocket as she gazed at the lawman.

'Hopefully, they'll want to avoid us,' she said and swung astride, turned north-easterly and riding slowly again on a loose rein, left Evan to follow. The only sound was made by their horses walking over ageless layers of brittle fir needles. Evan left the sign reading to the girl, he kept his head up searching for other forms of life, two-legged or four-legged.

The buckskin horse seemed to understand he was supposed to move slowly. He only responded to the occasional touch of reins. Evan brought up the rear, watching and only occasionally looking down. He rarely saw anything that might be a mark made by a shod horse and the farther they rode the more impressed he was with Lee Bovard's talent; that Navajo woman must have been a good teacher.

Lee drew rein near a craggy bluff and spoke from the saddle. 'He's paralleling the stage road northward.'

Evan nodded. 'Cloverdale?'

'Maybe. He might not continue northward. Let's go.'

The sun was hot on the rock bluff where neither trees nor brush grew, but the trail only skirted that way until the fugitive swung back into the forest. She spoke without looking up. 'He went over to that bluff to see below and behind.'

Where the trail crossed long areas of ground covered by years of needles Lee made good time, imprints were discernible where the weight of a horse crushed the fresher topmost layer and sank into the bone-dry needles below. Evan could make out most tracks until they were back among forest giants, then between gloom and fresher layers of fir needles he could not.

Eventually he made no attempt to read the sign. He alternately studied the areas they passed through and only occasionally watched the girl ahead, and once he saw a moving shadow and palmed his Colt. It wasn't a hide-out it was something more fearsome: a large, slick, black sow bear on her hind legs wrinkling her nose. She had their scent, at least the scent of their horses.

She had twin cubs no larger than small dogs. Evan called ahead. 'Sow bear with cubs,' and Lee boosted the buckskin into a lope.

The bear rooted with her nose. Evan hoped hard she would not catch sight of movement. Bears had poor eyesight.

The sow growled, her babies came close enough to touch her and the sow dropped down on all fours to lead her cubs in the opposite direction.

Evan leathered his six-gun as Lee slackened and rode from side to side searching for tracks. When she found them they led to a treeless clearing where a creek ran. Here, she sat still for a long time before saying, 'Watered his horse, spat out that jerky in the grass and kept on going.' She twisted in the saddle. 'How far have we come?'

He made a rangeman's guess, 'Six or seven miles.'

'Where is Cloverdale from here?'

Evan raised an arm. 'North-east.' He lowered the arm and also said, 'I know, it's slow going, but I'd a lot better arrive there late gettin' there by heading straight, than maybe end up losing him because he changed direction.'

She did not respond as they resumed their way. Where they stopped to water the horses she said, 'Something the old woman told me; following tracks makes you always behind. To catch someone you ought to be in front.'

He neither agreed nor disagreed and although he shared her impatience he simply rebridled his horse, mounted and continued in the direction they'd been riding. She loped ahead, resumed her position in front and only halted again when the sun they couldn't see had to be on its descent because the timber gloom was deepening, mostly on the far sides or trees and they had an unexpected encounter as they were crossing one of those small clearings. A loose horse raised its head where it had been grazing. Behind his right ear no more than five or six inches a feather had been braided into the mane.

Evan said, 'Hold up,' and they sat still exchanging stares with the loose horse. Lee finally dismounted but Evan remained astride, again holding his Colt just below the saddle swells in his lap.

They were deep into the wild primitive country and somewhere they could hear water running. It was a long wait before the Indian appeared. He was neither young nor old. He was fully clothed in a buckskin hunting shirt which reached almost to his knees with britches to match. He came soundlessly and slowly from the forest gloom northward carrying a brass-shiny Remington rifle.

He stopped well clear of the shadows, stood still and erect for a long time before moving closer. The rifle hung loose from one hand. His belt-knife had a forked antler for a handle. He looked steadily at Evan ignoring Lee. Somewhere a bird sounded loudly. It was a distraction but neither Evan nor Lee Bovard looked away from the Indian. He grounded his rifle and said, 'You lost?'

Evan answered. 'Not lost, tracking a bad man.'

'He pass when the sun was half rising.' The Indian raised one arm. 'Toward there.' He was pointing north-easterly. 'How bad you want him?'

'Real bad. I'm the law from Rock City.'

'What did he do?'

'Tried to kill me. Got others to steal cattle. Shot a boy in the back.' It wasn't quite the truth; Ordway hadn't shot Bovard's boy, but without question he would have.

The Indian loosened his stance but not his expression. 'You been up here before?'

'Never.'

'Other white men coming?'

'No. An' as far as we're concerned we didn't see no In'ian.'

Again the tomahawk raised one arm,

this time pointing directly northward. 'In'ian camp. You ridin' straight to it.'

Evan understood; the Indian had been sent to see if he and Lee Bovard would continue in the same direction or change course. They hadn't changed course. Evan ran a slow gaze among the huge trees, now in deep shadows, saw nothing, no movement of any kind and brought his gaze back to the Indian. 'The man we're after — did he ride to your camp?'

'No. We set three wolves on him. He cut that way, east.'

'You didn't stop him? He didn't see you?'

'He rode hard. Tame wolves. If he shot one we would have shot him.' The Indian hoisted the rifle into the crook of one arm. 'We want to set wolves to scare your horses too, but first we had to know if more whites coming.'

'Like I told you,' Evan replied. 'We're the only ones after that renegade bastard,' and when Lee swiftly looked around Evan understood. They had told the Indian they were alone, that there would be no more whiteskins in their wake.

The Indian looked in the direction from which he had come, faced forward and said, 'You ride far east. Mile east. You see nothing. You can find tracks go northward. Man you want is going north.'

They watched the Indian walk back in the direction or the trees and disappear. Lee dryly said, 'A mile eastward,' mounted her horse and led the way. Evan searched for movement where the Indian had disappeared, saw nothing and with the hair rising on the back of his neck followed Lee among more huge old trees, continued to follow her eastward until they reached a high bluff of solid tan stone where she stopped to ask if they'd covered a mile. He thought they had so when she led off again they went westerly to try and find Ordway's tracks again.

Oncoming dusk was against them but

Lee dismounted and led her horse, in places bending low but never faltering. Evan was more than just impressed.

When it became too dark Lee stopped where an old burn had left forest skeletons. There was a creek and tall grass. Where they hobbled the horses Evan lingered among big trees watching and waiting. Lee joined him. She had cleaned up at the creek and held out what had once been some kind of berry pie. He thanked her, took it and ate. She did the same except that she ate a strip of smoked meat. When he looked at her, she said, 'I don't like blueberry pie,' and watched the tired animals roll and graze; as she chewed meat.

He asked if she'd made the pie. She had, and although she had known it would never survive the trip to this place, she also knew that men liked blueberry pie. For a fact Evan Stannard did.

She gave it as her opinion that the hide-outs would not steal their horses and while he nodded as he ate, he would not have bet a lead cartwheel she was right.

'You told them we hadn't seen any Indians. You couldn't have done anything better to be sure they won't set us afoot.'

They returned where the saddlebags, saddlery and bedrolls were, did not make a fire and relaxed. Eventually the lawman said, 'I never seen anyone who could read sign like you can.'

She gazed out where the horses were indistinct when she spoke. 'The boys used to make fun of me for that, but my uncle gave me a silver bridle one time for tracking three horsethieves.'

'Hanged 'em, did he?'

The answer was delayed. 'No, he figured to. He was mad as hell. One of them was the son of the woman who taught me to track. He said a horsethief is a horsethief even if he's the son of the President of the United States.'

'Did he hang them anyway?'

'No. I said if he did that I'd leave and never want to look at him again.' She swung to face the marshal showing that fleeting smile, rueful this time. 'He took his quirt an' whipped their legs until they couldn't walk straight.'

From somewhere behind them in darkness it sounded like a muffled laugh. Lee swung her head but Evan didn't. 'A coyote,' he said.

She settled forward. 'You know better, coyotes don't live in forests.'

She unrolled her bedroll, kicked out of her boots, tossed her hat aside, crown down, and put the six-gun no more than six or eight inches from her head.

She looked steadily at Evan, who continued to sit against his bedroll. She said, 'Don't worry about the horses,' and he replied tartly. 'You got any idea how far it is back down out of here on foot?'

She didn't answer.

9

New Country

When he awakened the horses were out there grazing. He arose to find water and clean up. As he was returning he saw Lee in the middle of the small clearing talking to a tall Indian who had not only a cabine and a shell-belted pistol, but a big wicked looking fleshing knife.

As Evan approached Lee jutted her chin in his direction and said, 'Lawman Evan.'

The buck considered Evan impassively, he was older than the Indian they'd encountered the previous day and although his hair was braided there was no coup-feather. His name was Binjimin. He'd escaped from the Indian school in Arizona Territory many years earlier. He said he could speak English but he thought it was an ugly language. He also said he'd been sent by his tribal council to help track the fugitive renegade.

He returned to the camp with them, declined to eat and hunkered in brightening shadows watching the white-eyed people. He had tattoos, one across his dark forehead — an eagle in full flight, another one of a spider on the back of his right hand.

Evan explained that they did not need a tracker and bobbed his head in Lee's direction. The Indian stared, looked away then returned his doubting gaze back to Lee. She smiled but did not speak.

Lee and Evan exchanged a long glance, their thoughts similar, Binjimin was going to stay with them like it or not.

When they broke camp Lee showed Binjimin the sign and he went ahead of the horses, sometimes in a trot. Lee told Evan Binjimin was a better sign reader than she was, which appeared to be the truth. He only occasionally barely hesitated and when the sign was good he covered ground faster than a horse could walk.

The sun was directly overhead when Binjimin topped out where some prehistoric upthrust had rolled molten rock back upon itself. He stood like a statue. When Lee and the marshal came up they halted and sat still. In the middle distance of a large grassland plain was a village. Sunlight reflected and spirals of lazy smoke arose from buildings. Binjamin spoke without looking around.

'He went there.'

Evan nodded. Cloverdale was neither as large nor as thriving as Rock City, it was isolated from all outside influence excepting the coach road, and even that seemed to only make a brief sashay into the village then out the north end where it resumed its way arrow-straight into the distance.

Evan dismounted, fished forth several silver cart-wheels and handed them to the Indian as he said, 'We saw no In'ians,' and smiled. Binjimin remained expressionless but his dark eyes with their muddy whites showed a hint of dry humour. He grasped Evan between the wrist and elbow, removed his hand and without so much as a glance at Lee, went trotting back the way he had come.

Lee watched him leave and said, 'They're all alike, his kind or Navajo. A woman can't be their equal.'

As Evan moved to mount he said, 'An old man once told me mankind's troubles began when they figured to treat women as equals.'

She looked steadily at him until the horses were moving, made a derisive grunt, pushed ahead and picked up the sign on the downward side of that rolled-back tan bluff.

Ordway's tracks skirted around the bluff, joined a dusty game trail and went downhill for a mile until the game trail went one way, the tracks went another way and eventually reached the roadway; from there they went toward Cloverdale but because the road had many tracks she had to select only the most recent ones and even then because most sign was of shod horses she had to guess, which wasn't necessary until they reached the turnoff, then she slackened, leaned slightly until she was satisfied which were Ordway's marks, and picked them out among the other tracks.

On the outskirts of Cloverdale some ambitious soul with misplaced foresight had constructed a grain silo. In its dilapidated state it stood as the village's marker.

No one had broken the ground for many years, therefore the silo's builder had had no grain to store. It was good ground, the kind farmer-settlers would ordinarily develop, but settlers had not turned the earth for whatever reason. The silo's builder had abandoned his dream, moved on, leaving behind his out-of-place tall round wooden silo.

Otherwise the village was not

noticeable; there were about two dozen residences, a wide main road and three or four stores of which the most prominent was an emporium. Its owner did well, the nearest general store was southward at Rock City, a long and arduous distance.

There was no livery barn; there was a large public corral made of draw-knifed logs, badly cribbed but capable of holding animals. Evan and Lee Bovard were dumping their outfits when an old man accompanied by a too-fat collie dog came from one of the houses to greet them. He hadn't shaved in weeks. His eyes were brightly weasel-like. He said he had shucked hay and would feed their animals for fifteen cents a day. Evan handed him several coins and he departed followed by the old dog.

There was a café, as dilapidated as the abandoned silo. The proprietor was an elderly, square-built woman with pale-blue eyes, who made quilts. She hadn't had strangers in her little building in weeks. She brightened at their arrival, agreed to feed them and from her cooking area called questions. Were the strangers from Rock City? Why were they in Cloverdale? 'Passing through,' Evan said. When she brought their platters and coffee, she sat on a stool opposite them and said, if they were husband and wife why wasn't Lee wearing a wedding ring?

Evan reddened, ate and did not respond. Lee did; she said they were brother and sister not married folks, and headed off more questions by asking the elderly woman who ran cattle hereabouts.

The woman wagged her head. 'They come in summer, graze off and leave. Used to be a family named Argyle who lived out a few miles who ran livestock, but they pulled stakes and left years ago.'

Lee tried another tack. 'There are rangemen hereabouts, aren't there?'

The old woman's pale eyes seemed to narrow slightly with caution as she replied, 'There's the McDermot boys, they buy'n sell, an' trap mustangs.'

Evan picked up the conversation at this point. 'They been here long?'

'Yes, even before I come years ago. Old man McDermot died off a few years back. His boys taken over. They go on buyin' trips when they're after cattle, otherwise they trap horses.'

'You know 'em, do you, ma'am?'

'Known 'em since their ma stuffed moss in their pants. She upped and died too, three, four years back. Her name was Henrietta. She was from back East somewhere. She'n me made quilts an' crocheted things.'

'You remember the boys' names, ma'am?'

The old woman hadn't been shown respect in years. The man across the counter from her addressed her respectfully. She ignored Lee, put her full attention on Evan as she said, 'There's Jacob, he's the oldest. Then there's Caleb, next oldest and Samuel. Years back there was another one,

Artemus, but he wasn't a McDermot. He moved in out there, stayed three, four years and went on. A drifter, I'd say. Had a Texas accent. Local folks didn't take to him much. Was short with folks.'

'Has he been back?' Evan asked and the old woman's reply was short. 'Landsakes, no. He left before the old man died, must be ten, twelve years ago.'

Lee finished her meal, showed the quick, fleeting smile as she complimented the old woman on the meal, then asked directions to the McDermot place.

The old woman wasn't used to praise either; she blushed and offered them more coffee. She said if they figured to stay a while she'd make a cobbler.

Lee said they might be around a few days and if they were they'd look forward to the cobbler, and arose. 'How far is the McDermot place, ma'am?'

The 'ma'am' wasn't the same coming from the girl as it had been coming from her companion. The old woman returned her gaze to Evan when she answered.

'Three, four miles north-west. Over across the coach road an' up-country a piece. There's a big rock with a brand painted on it — turkey track. It's on the north side of the road leading to the McDermot place. You cattle buyers? I never met a woman cow buyer before.'

As Evan arose and spilled coins atop the counter he smiled at the old woman. 'Horse buyers, ma'am. An' we're obliged.'

Outside the day was wearing along. There were cottonwood trees on the east side of Cloverdale. Evan thought they should make camp and they went to get their bedrolls. The old man who had forked loose hay to their animals was leaning on the corral. The old dog was sitting beside him. When Evan and Lee came up, the old man turned. 'I know that Three Bells brand,' he said. 'It belongs to a man named Sam Bovard. His ranges come within a few miles of Cloverdale, at the foot of the bad country between. Is one of you a Bovard?'

Lee's response was cautious. 'That Three Bells brand is on a lot of animals. Sam Bovard is dead. His son has the place now.'

The old man looked surprised. 'You don't say. I never heard he had a son, but then I never knew Mister Bovard, just from what I heard.'

Lee's distraction had been successful. The old man related things he had heard about Sam Bovard and forgot altogether his earlier question about the Three Bells horse.

They took their bedrolls to the far side of the village, found a lively creek among the cottonwoods and made a dry camp. Lee said, 'The trail's getting warm.'

Evan answered while unrolling the bedroll, 'Artemus?'

Lee laughed. 'I once knew a woman named Frank. Ordway knows us both by sight.'

Evan coiled his shell-belt with the holstered Colt on top, put his hat aside upside down, and plucked a grass stalk as he lay back.

'Scout up the place. If it's open country stay a long way out. If he's there, we got to see him.'

'And?'

'Tomorrow night ride close, go ahead on foot, kick the door open an' anyone who reaches for a gun, shoot him.'

Lee sat cross-legged atop her bedroll. 'And if he's not there?'

'If he's been there talk to his friends.'

Lee sighed. 'I hope he's there, not gone off maybe to Colorado or some place a long way from here.'

'Go to sleep.'

'Do you like cobbler?'

He sat up looking at her. 'Apple cobbler. I didn't see no apple trees.'

'Cobblers can be made from raisins. I've seen them made from rhubarb.'

His eyes widened. 'Rhubarb cobbler? It'd be as bitter as sin.'

'Not if it's made with lots of sugar.'

He sank back.

She spoke again. 'I can make an apple cobbler that'd melt in your mouth.'

This time when he spoke he did not raise up, he simply said, 'You cook, read sign, what else can you do?'

She got comfortable in her bedroll and did not say another word.

They struck camp before sunrise, left Cloverdale by the stage road bundled into their coats. If anyone saw them leave it had to be the old man who brought a huge forkful of hay to pitch to their horses, otherwise there wasn't a light among the houses nor anyone abroad.

They found the turkey-track rock with a reddish sun rising, rode past it for a mile then swung westerly.

Distant cattle were bawling, mammy cows who couldn't find their calves. Evan set a course in that direction. They could see no buildings for an excellent reason, in flat country where wind was a genuine curse, humans sought broad arroyos for their

181

buildings. They saw bands of cattle, avoiding crowding close in order to avoid a stampede and stopped when they topped out over a wide swale where a creek ran. There were cattle down. Evan estimated maybe a hundred head. Mostly they were cows with calves.

One old brockle-faced girl with a gawky calf threw up her head and faced around. She had caught the scent first. When she turned she saw the pair of riders motionless atop the landswell. Prompted by instinct she began to sidle among the other animals, bumping them out of her way. The baby calf followed but not handily. It was only a day old.

Most of the cattle were at the creek to drink. They ignored the wary brockle-faced cow.

Lee said, 'They've evidently been buying cattle. That bunch at the creek plus other bands we've seen add up to quite a herd.'

Evan said nothing, he was watching the skittish old girl with the day-old calf. If anything could start a stampede it would be old brockle-face. He reined northward with Lee following, which checkmated the cow's move to get away. He rode slowly, almost as though he hadn't understood what the old cow had in mind. She stopped, head high, watched for a moment then rattled her horns. Evan kept on riding northward along the landswell. He did not change course until the brockle-faced cow had decided there was no danger and turned back toward the creek, when her rear end was higher than her head as she drank, Evan changed course riding westerly. Once, the cow threw up her head dripping water, then lowered it. She knew from experience riders were a problem only when they tried to get close. These horsemen were a considerable distance and were now riding westerly.

She went back to drinking.

Evan changed course again, southward this time and while all the cattle had seen the horsemen by now, they simply watched them. Not until Evan reined eastward and slightly northward did the cattle show nervousness. The brockle-faced old girl pushed through southward, halted clear of her companions, ducked her head and pawed. Her earlier fear had become something else, she flung dirt and rattled her horns; she was ready to fight. Nothing fights quicker than a cow with a baby calf.

Evan pushed ahead with care and reined to a stop when the other cattle began bawling and milling. He and the brockle-faced cow looked steadily at one another. Lee eased up beside Evan. While the stand-off continued she quietly said, 'Notice anything, Evan?'

His reply was just as quiet. 'Yeah. That old girl and the line-backed cow behind her got a Three Bells brand on the right side and what looks like a bird track on the left side.' He looked at the woman beside him. 'How long did Ordway work for old Sam?'

'I don't know. About six or seven

years maybe. Why?'

'That brockle-faced cow's at least nine years old. She's got the horns of Texas-bred animals. Old Sam bred up and culled close. Want me to guess?'

'Yes.'

'Ordway stole off Three Bells for a long time. A few head now an' then.'

Lee was briefly quiet before speaking again. 'Let's go back to Cloverdale.'

He looked surprised. 'We ain't found the buildings yet.'

She raised an arm. 'Bawling cattle get attention.'

They couldn't make out the riders but the dust they kicked up spiralled into the fresh morning.

Evan turned and led off in a lope. When he could no longer see the dust he slackened to a walk and said, 'Ma'am, just for the hell of it let's assume at least one of 'em's as good a tracker as you are.'

She was looking over her shoulder when she replied, 'Remember me telling you what the Navajo woman taught me?'

'About tracking?'

'No; about people who track other people are always behind them.' She faced forward, with the stage road in sight she also said, 'We go north up the road, it's full of tracks. Go north a long way, then cut west. If they're in Cloverdale and don't find anything, they'll head back, and we'll already be back there, ahead of them.'

He stared. 'I'll even eat your rhubarb cobbler.'

When they reached the road they went northward. This time they were farther north than they had been when they'd left the road about sunrise. This time they were in country neither of them had ever seen before and while it was the same grassland, it had undulations, some of them broad and deep enough to hide someone on horseback, and it also had occasional bosques of trees.

Lee came up atop a gradual landswell

186

where the far side sloped down into one of those wide, deep and grassy arroyos. She rode downward and reined southward. They would not be visible unless pursuers tracked them and found the arroyo. It was a risk, she said, but not a great one. Unless there was a good tracker among their pursuers they wouldn't be able to read sign for the miles up the stage road where they had left it riding west.

Lee's confidence was deserved except for one thing. When their pursuers entered Cloverdale there would be at least one old man with a collie dog and an old woman who made quilts between visitors to her eatery who would be able to describe Lee Bovard and Marshal Stannard.

Evan did not think of this as he followed the buckskin horse. It only occurred to him when their arroyo began to gradually rise up toward the level countryside, and they stopped. He said, 'They'll know who we are an' do their damnedest to find us. They'll scour the range.'

Lee sat eyeing the countryside. 'Find another gully goin' southward.'

They had to cross open country for more than a mile before they found what they were looking for. The difference with the next arroyo was that it had flourishing trees and undergrowth on both sides of a creek and while this impeded progress it gave them an opportunity to water and rest the horses. While they were doing this Lee asked a question that had nothing to do with their present position. She said, 'Why aren't you married?'

They were sitting beside the creek in tree shade. Evan flipped a stone into the water to cover his surprise. Eventually he said, 'I can't rightly say.'

'You've known women you liked, haven't you?'

He flicked another stone. 'I expect so. If this gully runs far enough south we could maybe see the buildings.'

188

She said, 'I'm hungry?' and that rattled him too. 'Drink water?' he said, and tossed another stone in the creek. 'Personally, I could sleep until tomorrow.'

A pair of nesting birds frantically scolded from up in their tree. One, probably the male bird, even made a daring swoop close enough for Lee to duck. Evan lay back and a bee came out of nowhere and stung his neck. He sat up stifling curses. Lee found the stinger and removed it. Evan stood up. 'I don't like this place?' he said and went after his horse.

Lee didn't move as she watched him. When he leaned to remove the hobbles she said, 'They haven't grazed long enough?' and he straightened up without touching the hobbles.

She was as handsome a woman as he had ever seen, and she could do things he'd never known another woman could do, but there was something about her . . .

He hunkered where the horses were

picking with his back to her and remained that way until she came along, knelt, drank at the creek and arose facing him. 'It bothers you as a man to have a woman make suggestions, doesn't it?'

He arose, looked out of the arroyo seeking shadows and when he saw them he squatted to remove the hobbles. This time she followed his example, also without speaking.

The arroyo had reason to be miles long; as a watercourse that had carved its pathway for more years than either of the riders following it southward could have imagined, it had groped and twisted for many miles and would continue to do, again, for longer than the pair of riders could imagine.

10

Snakes and Guns

Neither of them would forget this arroyo, not entirely because they encountered a large female rattlesnake with her inchling babies crawling over her and everything else they encountered, but because the snake went into an instantaneous quivering coil, tail up and rattling, head sucked back to strike, and Lee's buckskin horse bogged his head, threw her into a thicket and turned to bolt past Evan who barely had time to lean far out and grab one flying rein.

The buckskin's momentum yanked Evan out of the saddle. He held tightly to the rein. Not until the buckskin had run into a massive thicket, between the thicket and the man on the end of one braided rawhide rein, could the horse be stopped. He was shaking and wild-eyed. Evan could not lead him back; he tried several times before tying the horse in the thicket to go back where his own animal was standing as though he neither knew what a rattlesnake was, which was improbable, or had any fear of one.

Lee climbed out of the thicket which had broken her fall and was reaching for her six-gun when Evan yelled and lunged at her, caught her gun-wrist and twisted it until she dropped the gun.

As he released her he said, 'The noise would travel miles.'

She looked behind him where the mother snake was no longer rattling but still had her head cocked back to strike.

Evan threw his hat, the snake struck, he grabbed the hat with fangs through it, flung the hat away and stood with his back to Lee until the snake got disentangled and slid among some rocks.

When he came back from retrieving

the hat Lee said, 'It's dripping.'

Venom dripped from inside the hat. Evan eyed the hat and softly swore, knelt, got soft earth and scrubbed inside his hat.

Lee sat on a rock neither moving nor speaking. When he arose to punch the hat back into shape she stared at him. 'No one told me he's afraid of snakes,' she said, arose from the rock and winced.

He asked if she was hurt. Her answer was short. 'Of course not; how could anyone get bucked off a horse and land in some kind of stickery bushes and be hurt?'

He went after the buckskin. When he led it back it resisted every step. He finally halted, told Lee to come toward him and when she did he handed her the reins. 'We'll ride down the creek,' he said, mounted his animal and turned back.

A mile farther along out of the creek riding southward she said, 'I apologize.'

He did not respond, there was grit inside his hat and the buckskin had jerked him so abruptly from the saddle his arm and shoulder were painful.

There was silence between them until the arroyo widened and the creek made a pool. Several horses were drinking. At the sight of riders they tucked tail and ran. Lee said, 'Mustangs.'

Evan looked straight at her. 'Did you ever see a branched mustang? Those were turkey track horses.' He faced forward. 'We're gettin' close.'

The buckskin hiked along with his ears pointing and his neck cocked slightly to one side. Horses that are terrified of snakes, particularly the rattling kind, do not recover from encounters for many hours.

In the arroyo, a combination of water and heat ensured high humidity. People and horses sweated. Neither Lee Bovard nor the marshal did nothing more to acknowledge humidity than to occasionally wipe their faces and necks. At one place on the far southerly edge of the pool Evan dismounted, knelt and scrubbed the inside of his hat. Lee watched impassively. After total immersion and scrubbing the hat was shapeless. When Evan put it on if the circumstances had been different Lee would have laughed.

She had stickers in the back and sides of her shirt. She also had a sore hip. She would have died before mentioning these things as the wringing wet buckskin followed Evan's horse.

He was not uncomfortable about being short with her, but he did look back once and say, 'Good odds, two cripples against whatever's ahead.'

She forced a smile. 'Lead on, Lochinvar.'

'Who the hell is Lochinvar?'

'My hero when I was young . . . it's a story in a book.'

He missed the innuendo because the arroyo was beginning to lose its trees and brush. He could see well ahead and there were two horsemen in the distance. 'Company,' he told her, and swung down to lead the horse. Mounted people made excellent targets. He was unaware that as she followed she favoured one leg.

The horsemen appeared to be divided in their attention. They watched the arroyo and the easterly area. Evan had no illusions. When the cover diffused further he stopped, watched the riders, then tied his animal to a spindly pine, took down his Winchester and went ahead from shadow to bush. Lee came behind also with her saddle gun.

The unexpected occurred. They saw a clutch of buildings in the distance. Evidently the creek ran that far and farther. It would be the source for water where those buildings stood with creek willows and a number of unkempt old cottonwoods.

Evan paused beside some kind of flourishing big bush with small pale flowers and ignored the bees circulating among the flowers. When Lee came up Evan said, 'If that's the McDermot place we're in luck,' and ignored her dour response: 'If that's the McDermot place we'll need more than luck.'

The riders split up, one started out and around the east side of the arroyo, the other came directly toward it. When he was close enough his appearance was unmistakably hostile.

He was a greying, lean, rawboned man with a prominent hawk-like nose and a wound for a mouth. He had a saddle gun under the fender of his saddle on the right side and wore a shell-belt and holstered Colt, also on the right side, and although his saddle was old and worn his horse was slick and breedy looking.

Lee started to speak. Evan silenced her before she could say more than a couple of words and motioned for her to follow his example as he utilized every inch of the cover provided by the flowering large bush.

Whoever the rider was, he was no greenhorn. He passed silently into the arroyo where the ground was marshy, reins in the left hand, right hand inches above the hip holster from which the tie-down had been yanked loose.

Except for movement the man's approach would not have been noticeable. He halted in the dappled shade of a tree evidently to listen as well as look. When he resumed his advance the only time he averted his head was once, when he got rid of a cud of tobacco.

Evan drew his handgun. The rider would pass within a couple of yards of their concealing bush. He would see their horses. In fact when he was abreast of their bush one of the horses flung its head and stamped at deer flies and the horseman became a statue.

Evan eased bushes aside, raised his weapon and cocked it. The mounted man's reaction was instantaneous, he swung off on the right side of his mount with only his legs and hat showing.

Evan did not raise his voice. 'Don't even breathe.'

The rawboned man slapped his horse on the rump and fired at the same time. The diversion didn't work as it was supposed to. Evan fired holding the gunbarrel low.

The stranger's bullet tore through the big bush and made Lee wince. For a sound shot it was very close. The rawboned man fell with blood appearing on his lower trouser leg. He fired again, too fast this time, the slug went high overhead.

Evan called out, 'You're a dead target. Shuck the gun.'

The rawboned older man, obviously a seasoned gunman, hadn't lived as long as he had by not also being capable of cold reasoning. He dropped the gun, leaned to use both hands to grip the bleeding leg. Without taking his eyes off the wounded man Evan told Lee to go catch his horse. When she emerged from the thicket the older man's eyes followed her until Evan stood up to push clear of the thicket and approach the stranger, this time the wounded man's eyes never left the marshal.

Evan said, 'Take off your belt an' tie it tight above the blood.'

The older man did exactly that. If there was pain, and there had to be, when he raised his eyes to Evan it did not show. He said, 'Who the hell are you? And the woman?'

Evan ignored the look and the question, moved behind the wounded man, put his pistol barrel into the man's ear and groped for other weapons. He found two, one was a short-barrelled, nickel-plated .41 calibre derringer, the other was a boot-knife sharp enough to shave with. Evan hurled them away, pushed on the gun barrel and asked the stranger his name.

'Jacob McDermot. What's yours?'

'Evan Stannard.'

'The lawman from down at Rock City,' McDermot said and it was a statement not a question.

'Where's Tex?'

'He's around. Mister, you're bottled up in this gully. They've heard them guns for five miles.' McDermot paused to watch Lee Bovard lead back his breedy horse. It had a turkey track brand on the left shoulder. McDermot said, 'Is that your deputy? Must be hard up to find 'em down in Rock City.'

'Tighten the belt,' Evan said, and McDermot leaned to obey. There had been blood trickling. He asked if Evan had a knife. 'I got to punch another hole in the belt.'

Evan dropped his clasp knife and McDermot picked it up, flicked open a blade and went to work making the hole. Evan moved the gun barrel to McDermot's back and pushed. McDermot made the hole, pushed the tongue through and hurled Evan's knife into the creek. 'They told us in Cloverdale who you was. Marshal, you don't have the chance of a snowball in hell.'

Lee tied the wounded man's horse, splashed across the creek and was climbing up the easterly bank of soft, crumbly earth when a man yelled at her and fired. Her reaction surprised both Marshal Stannard and his prisoner, she twisted and fired at the same time. The man above the arroyo on the east side bawled like a bay steer, rolled over the edge and fell all the way to the creek. Lee limped over where he was clawing mud to reach the verge. When he looked up her six-gun barrel was no more than three feet away cocked and aimed.

The wounded man said, 'Who is that, Annie Oakley?'

Evan's answer prevented the wounded man from speaking for a long time. 'Lee Bovard. She's niece to James Bovard.'

'Sam Bovard?'

'James, his son.'

'I didn't know Sam had a son.'

'Old Sam's dead, his son runs the outfit. I'd've thought Tex would have told you James Bovard killed Sam.'

'Never mentioned it,' McDermot said, watching a mud-encrusted man stand up at the edge of the creek and said, 'That's Sam, my youngest brother. He couldn't shoot a hole in a barn from the inside.' As Lee herded the youngest McDermot, also tall but with a childlike face, where McDermot and the marshal were, the youngest McDermot said, 'You told me a woman couldn't hit a tree two feet away.'

There was blood dripping from Sam McDermot's right sleeve. Lee told him to sit down, which he did looking sullenly at his brother. 'I was propped up to shoot again. She shot the damned arm out from under me.'

Sam looked from Lee to his brother and shook his head.

Lee used the same technique, a trouser belt, to cinch off Sam McDermot's wounded arm and she was not gentle. Sam probably would have cried out anyway. From Evan's position behind the eldest McDermot, Sam appeared to be in his twenties, well past the age most men shaved but his face was as smooth as a spanked baby's bottom.

When Lee finished, the bleeding had stopped but Sam groaned, rocked back and forth and glared at his brother.

Lee was looking at the wounded men when she said, 'Evan, I'd take it kindly if you'd fetch the horses. My right leg hurts.'

Because she hadn't mentioned being injured before, Evan stared. She spoke again, irritably this time. 'I'd like to rest here for a while, but if there are more of 'em they sure as hell heard gunfire.'

After Evan departed to find the animals Jacob McDermot said, 'You don't look like old Sam but you sure got the same grit in your craw.'

Lee eased down holding her cocked pistol loosely. As she studied the hawk-faced older man she said, 'How long have you an' Tex Ordway been stealing Three Bells' cattle?'

McDermot returned Lee's gaze without blinking. 'Where'd you ever get that notion?'

She raised the six-gun. 'How long,

you rustling son of a bitch? I'd as soon blow your head off as look at you.'

The large baby-faced man said, 'Tell her for Chris'sake, Jake.'

McDermot replied quietly, 'Somethin' like six, eight years ma'am,' and smiled.

She lowered the gun as Evan returned with the horses, got up, flinched and went to help him. As she faced the marshal she quietly said, 'There are trees back a-ways, Marshal.'

Evan fumbled a bridle and had to lower it for a better grip.

She said, 'Well? It's that or turn them loose, isn't it?'

'No, ma'am, we'll take 'em along with us an' ride to that ranch down yonder. If the other two are down there we got shields.'

She said no more but when Evan growled for the McDermots to get a-horseback she eyed them both darkly.

As they left the arroyo and widened the distance between themselves and the creek, Evan asked Jacob McDermot if that was his home place and the older man nodded without speaking. He had his jaws clamped, every step of the breedy horse shot pain through him. When Evan asked if Ordway and his other brother would be there, McDermot did not unlock his jaws, he simply shrugged.

If he'd spoken he could have saved Evan at least an hour of wary riding with the baby-faced McDermot in front of him as a shield. There were no gunshots and no one appeared in the yard but a black and white dog. It was a bitch. She stood in the centre of the yard wagging her tail without barking.

Evan led the way into the large old barn from out back, helped Jacob McDermot dismount and he fainted. The youngest McDermot glared and when Evan leaned to grip the unconscious man under both shoulders Sam growled, 'Leave him be. Maybe he'll bleed out or somethin'. Maybe the horses'll trample the bastard.'

Evan dragged McDermot over to a

closed stall and propped him there. Lee found an old lass rope. She and Evan trussed the unconscious man like a calf.

Sam said, 'Cal'll find him.'

Evan stood up regarding the unconscious man. It was Lee who thought they should put him inside the stall with a door, which they did, and covered him with loose hay.

Sam had a remark to make about that too. 'Maybe he'll smother in there.'

They closed the stall door, got its hasp in place and faced the baby-faced large man with the bloody sleeve and sullen eyes.

Sam said, 'I been tellin' Jake all year someone's goin' to make a gather, come up missin' some an' come over here. You can't tell Jake anythin'. He's like Pa was.'

They herded Sam in the direction of the house from behind. The only thing that happened was when the black and white dog came up and jumped on Sam. His expression changed as he leaned to stroke the dog. 'Ma'am, you got a dog?'

'We have a ranch dog.'

Sam was straightening up when he said, 'They're better'n people, aren't they?'

There was no one in the house but there had been and when they had left they must have been in a hurry because the door was wide open. Evan told Sam where to sit. The house was large with a number of rooms, it was poorly lighted and strong smelling. Lee wrinkled her nose. 'Like a boar's nest,' she said. Evan left her to watch the retarded McDermot and prowled rooms until he found one that was an office. It was one of the most untidy rooms of the house.

He broke open a large drawer, lifted out two heavy ledgers and stood turning pages. He could not believe how meticulous one of the McDermots had been. There were pages listing bands of horses and herds of stolen cattle. They showed owners' brands and in red ink where the animals had been rebranded with the turkey track brand.

There were names and dates going back more than fifteen years, entries about long drives, wholesale lots of rebranded cattle and forged bills of sale.

He went to the parlour and jerked his head at Lee. 'Go in there; there's books of records. I'll watch Sam.'

She was gone a long time. Sam started talking, he was both sullen and resentful and he clearly did not like Jacob, the eldest McDermot.

'He cut corners when we divvied up. I know he did even though Cal said he didn't, an' he'd make me take the drag, knowin' damned well if we was follered I'd be the one got caught or shot.'

Evan examined the injured arm, loosened the belt until there was fresh bleeding then tightened it again. Sam tried to jerk away. 'What you doin' tryin' to bleed me out?'

Evan returned to his chair and

leaned forward. 'Tell me about your pa,' he said.

It was like opening a floodgate. 'Pa give me things. When I was big enough he give me a black pony, but Ma was my best friend. She wouldn't stand for the others raggin' me. I think it was my eighteenth birthday she died. She didn't have to do that, mister.'

Lee came from the untidy office with two ledger books. She said, 'Evan, after dark I think we'd ought to head for Rock City.'

Sam looked at her smiling. 'Rock City's got a real pretty girl named Samantha. I told Pa I figured to marry her, an' you know what he did? Sent me with Jake'n Cal on a drive up into Montana. It was colder'n hell. They ragged me all the way up an' on the cattle drive all the way back. I jumped Cal and Jake piled in. I got a good beatin'. Ma'am, do you know a girl named Samantha in Rock City?'

Lee put the ledgers aside and sat on a leather sofa to favour her sore leg and hip. 'I'm new to Rock City,' she told Sam, and he kept smiling.

'Samantha's as pretty as you. What's your name?'

'Lee Bovard.'

Sam softly frowned. 'Ain't Lee a man's name? My Pa used to tell us stories about a man he called Massa Bobby Lee. Pa was a soldier under him.'

Evan found a half-bottle of corn whiskey, took one swallow and took the bottle to Sam, who emptied the bottle without a pause.

They exchanged glances and Evan went out front to see if there were horsemen. There were none. He returned to the house as Sam McDermot slid from his chair to the floor making little puppy sounds.

Lee went to the kitchen.

11

Before Dawn

A meal helped but they were both dog-tired and bruised.

Lee was sceptical when Evan thought Ordway and the other McDermot would return. She said, 'Return from where?'

'Looking for us,' the marshal answered testily. 'Isn't that what this is all about?'

They ignored unkempt, bloody-armed Sam McDermot unconscious on the parlour floor and went down to the barn where Jacob had recovered and had been trying to gnaw his binding. He looked even dirtier and haggard than Sam had looked, but there was fire in his stare at them.

Evan knelt to examine the wound, which had become so swollen the belt was nearly out of sight. The light was not good; whether the woman and the marshal realized it, this day was drawing to a close.

Lee wrinkled her nose and left the stall to go out back where the air was pure. During her absence Evan told the hawk-faced man he needed a doctor and got a spiteful retort.

'Before I'm through with you, mister, you'll wish you was dead.'

Evan regarded the older man from an expressionless face. 'Where did your brother and Ordway go?'

'Lookin' for you'n her.'

'We'll be waitin,' Evan replied quietly. 'Better odds now. Sam's passed out on the floor in the house.'

Jacob McDermot spat venom. 'Pa should've got rid of him. We couldn't even trust him to go to Coverdale by hisself. He'd start talkin' to anyone he met about things Pa an' me told him never to talk about.'

'What's wrong with him?'

'He was born with both feet out of the stirrups. Ma knew it before the rest

213

of us, an' she favoured him all his damned life. Pa too, but only when he was young.'

Lee appeared in the stall doorway. 'A rider coming,' she told Evan and he left the hawk-faced man to go out back with her.

The solitary horseman was approaching at a slow walk. He was watching the yard. Lee sensed his tenseness. 'He's tracking us,' she said, and Evan nodded. She also said, 'I'll get my Winchester.'

Evan remained in the doorless, wide, rear barn opening. When Lee returned with a saddle gun he told her unless he was wrong there had to be two of them.

She said, 'Maybe,' and grounded the Winchester. 'In a few minutes he'll be in range.'

Evan looked at her and looked back out where the rider was clearly discernible even though dusk was beginning to settle. 'Wait,' he said. 'It could be a neighbour.'

She made a slight snorting sound of derision which Evan ignored.

From back inside the barn Jake McDermot called, 'The belt broke. It's bleedin' again.'

Lee appeared to be deaf. Evan returned to the stall and got a surprise. The eldest McDermot was standing up with all his weight on his good leg and holding a thick scantling in both hands. He swung with all his strength when Evan appeared in the doorway. If the blow had landed squarely it would have put the marshal face down, but he had about three seconds to take a backward step so that only the tip caught his shirt and tore it.

McDermot fumbled an effort to raise the scantling and the gunshot that nearly deafened Evan knocked McDermot against the stall wall to the point where the side wall joined the rear wall, and there he fell without a sound.

Lee Bovard cocked the gun for another shot.

Evan could make out the puckered hole in the back of McDermot's shirt, high up and said, 'He don't need another one.'

Without a word they returned to the rear barn opening where the distant rider had abruptly stopped. She spoke too softly for the marshal to hear when she said, 'A little closer, just a little closer.'

Shadows inside the barn had thickened to the point where it seemed unlikely that distant horsemen could see them.

Lee said, 'Tipped our hand, Evan. Whoever he is he's not going to keep coming.'

She was right but for a long time the horseman sat far out as motionless as a statue before reining westerly, still riding at a walk.

When she said she thought they could run that one down Evan shook his head. 'Let him bring the fight to us.'

Until dusk was fully settled they could see the rider. He did not deviate from his westerly course nor did he increase his gait.

Evan raised his disreputable hat, scratched and dropped it back down. If that had been a McDermot out yonder, and if Tex Ordway was also out there somewhere and had heard the gunshot, with the day dying around the yard either one of the men they were here to fight would shortly be provided with the best of all sources of protection to sneak into the yard — nightfall. If they met, and converged . . .

Lee forked hay to their horses, crossed the yard to the house and returned after a brief sojourn to inform Evan that Sam McDermot was still passed out. She handed him two slices of coarse-grained bread with a slab of cooked meat between.

As they ate dusk deepened into night and inside the barn where daylight never reached, the darkness was deepest. An owl abruptly drooped from the rafters and soundlessly winged its way out the front barn opening.

They saw it beat its wings in a scramble to gain altitude and lost sight of it. Lee made a quiet comment, 'Owls are secret people,' a comment Evan ignored; Indians, part-Indians and people who had lived among Indians attributed unprovable facts to most living creatures.

He was wiping both hands on his trouser leg when a rock landed in the centre of the earthen floor. Both he and Lee sat perfectly still, until Evan said, 'Pretty good toss for an owl.'

Lee arose to soundlessly approach the front barn opening. Evan watched; whoever or whatever had tossed the rock would be waiting for a reaction, particularly movement. Lee stopped well back from the opening.

Time passed, Evan arose from the small keg he had been sitting on and when Lee came back he softly said, 'He knows we're here. He tracked us from the arroyo. My guess is that he went around the yard looking for tracks that we'd left, and didn't find any.'

Lee said, 'He smokes,' and Evan made another deduction from that. 'If you could smell tobacco smoke he's in the yard. Watch out front, I'll watch out back.'

As Evan stood on the north side of the rear barn opening someone fired a gun into the barn. The slug went through from the front to the back. Evan knelt to block in squares of what he could see, and saw neither movement or anything that could be the shape of a man. He was shifting slightly to look northward when the second gunshot erupted, this time from somewhere in the darkness behind the barn.

There were two of them!

The silence returned for a while, until the sound of a door being opened and closed, suggested that at least one of their enemies had gone into the house. Evan thought that one would be the McDermot, which meant the second one was Tex Ordway.

He got belly down and squirmed

far enough forward to be able to see along the rear barn wall. Their corralled horses were standing like carvings, heads up, ears pointing southward.

Evan shifted position to look in that direction and saw a swift blur of movement where someone was clearly trying to reach a three-sided blacksmithing shed. He aimed his six-gun and waited, but the ghost was no longer visible. He thought about sound shooting into the shoeing shed and refrained because his handgun ammunition was limited.

A venomous voice called, 'All's we got to do, lawman, is set down an' wait. We got lots of time.'

Neither Lee nor Evan answered.

Evan strained to catch movement of the man in the shoeing shed, but whoever he was, he was no novice either. The man out front called again. He had a reedy voice. 'Lawman, where's Jacob?'

Evan did not reply, nor was he distracted from his vigil in the direction of the blacksmith shop. He knew who was in the shed: Tex Ordway. The reedy voice had a Texas accent.

Ordway called again, 'Come out without no guns, lawman. If you don't I'll burn the barn down on top of you.'

This time the gunshot came from inside the barn, up in the vicinity of the front opening. It was followed by the sound of someone falling but any hope the two in the barn might have derived from this was demolished when reedy-voice fiercely cursed a rock which had caused him to stumble when he leapt backwards.

Lee took advantage of the swearing to try a sound shot and she must have come close because the swearing man went silent as he threw a spiteful, unaimed shot back inside the barn. This slug shattered one of the boards in the door of the stall where dead Jake McDermot was lying.

For a long time there was not a sound. Evan continued to concentrate on the shoeing shed. What ultimately broke the silence was two close-spaced muffled gunshots inside the house.

Neither of the forted-up people in the barn could make sense of that noise. Neither believed the surviving McDermot had shot his passed-out brother. To Evan, the shots had sounded almost muffled, as though the shooter's gun barrel had been very close to its objective.

There were no echoes from inside the house. Lee inched forward to peek around the opening. The house was dark, the front door was open but there was no sign of anyone over there.

Evan briefly looked back up through the barn where he could barely make Lee out and hissed at her. 'Get the hell away from that opening!'

She walked the full distance of the barn and stopped near enough to Evan to speak but not near enough for whoever was in the shoeing shed to see her.

'Did you try to open that bottom

desk drawer?' she asked and before he could reply she also said, 'He shot the lock off.'

Evan craned around to look upwards. He had seen the lock on the drawer but after finding the ledgers he had ignored the drawer.

The same thought was in both their minds. Evan said, 'Find their horses, set them afoot.'

She did not say a word, but she leaned to peer at the shoeing shed. Evan said, 'It's got to be Ordway. He's in there. He hasn't come out.'

Lee straightened back. 'Where did they leave their horses?'

Evan had no idea. 'Out yonder somewhere.'

She raised her carbine as she said, 'Sluice the shed,' fired, levered up and fired again. Evan emptied his six-gun. There were sounds from inside the shed of bullets striking anvils, hanging tools, even the forge on its rock base.

When they had to reload Lee thought no man could have survived, but a solitary six-gun shot came from the shed and barely missed Lee Bovard. She dropped the Winchester, palmed her Colt and emptied it in the direction of the shed.

This time no one fired back and Lee showed Evan that quick fleeting smile. She was reloading from her shell belt when she said, 'Let's risk it,' and holstered the reloaded Colt.

The marshal, who was not a believer in odds, taking chances when they weren't necessary, shook his head.

She frowned. 'How else do we set them afoot?'

'If we got Ordway there's only one left. You hold a steady aim. I'm goin' to the north side of the shed. If he's able and tries a shot, empty your gun.'

She said, 'That's risky, Evan.'

He nodded in agreement, 'But necessary. I don't want to spend the rest of the night in this barn.'

Neither of them had noticed the faint chill which had come into the night.

Evan in particular was unaware of the passing time as he concentrated on reaching the north side of the smithy. If Ordway was still standing in the shed he gave no indication of having seen the dark moving shadow.

As Evan flattened against ancient warped wooden siding the only thing he heard was a pounding heart. His.

Someone at the house bellowed like a fighting bull and for as long as that noise lasted there was no activity.

Evan took a moment to speculate. If the retarded McDermot had made that noise it could mean his brother was over there with him, and that the slow-witted McDermot could have attacked his kinsman, an excellent probability since the big man had shown a fierce dislike of his brothers.

As Evan moved soundlessly along the shed's north wall Ordway bumped an anvil which made a pair of pincers fall. Evan wagged his head; only someone who was bulletproof could still be moving after all the lead that had been fired into the shed.

He got close enough to the front wall to stop and listen. Across the intervening distance Lee Bovard hissed. Evan flattened. That she had seen him moving was obvious. He glared in the dark. She was not visible, but inside the shed someone was moving.

If Evan had dared he would have cussed her out like she'd never been cussed at before. What she had done was make Ordway aware that he was being stalked.

The chill increased as did the deadly stillness. Evan waited to hear sounds from inside the shed. There was no sound.

He inched ahead until he could see the main house across the yard.

It was dark and silent. Evan used a cuff to dab at sweat before taking down a deep breath and holding it as he got down on one knee, raised his six-gun and eased forward. The inside of the shed was abysmally dark. Nothing moved. He eased ahead several inches, six-gun held high.

If Ordway was inside he had to be crouching, perhaps beside or behind the rock emplacement where the forge was. Evan leaned further with every instinct telling him to stop, which he did.

What changed everything was the sudden sound of a running horse. Before Evan straightened up Lee sprang into the wide doorless opening, six-gun up as she fired three times as rapidly as she could pull the trigger. She was fully exposed. Evan was poised to tell her to get out of sight when the unmistakable sound of a Winchester saddle gun drowned out the other sound. Evan saw both muzzleblasts. Whoever had shot back was riding in a belly-down race to get clear. Both slugs struck the front of the barn, close but not close enough.

Evan launched himself like a catapult, hit the girl high, knocking her violently backward into the floor. She made a strangling sound and fought like a

tiger until she saw Evan's face. As
she squirmed free she angrily said,
'You satisfied, you damned idiot! He
went out the back way of the shed, got
his horse, *you damned fool!*'

Evan disentangled himself, yanked
her to her feet and sucked clear of the
blow she threw. He caught her by the
shoulders, spun her and propelled her
violently forward until she fell. She lost
her gun, pushed clear of the earthern
floor and lunged for it.

Evan put his left foot on the gun and
leaned. He said, 'Get up!'

The running-horse sounds were no
longer audible. When they were face to
face she spat words. 'I'd like to know
how you've lived this long. Didn't you
see him go out the back way!'

Evan didn't reply. He had been
concentrating on the open front of
the shed.

'If you think I'm going to help you
run him down . . . ' she exclaimed, and
leaned to retrieve her six-gun as Evan
removed his foot from it. 'Didn't you

see him run out of there!'

Evan hadn't seen Ordway's departure, he had been concentrating on the front of the shed, not the back of it. She yelled at him. 'He could have shot you in the back!' She made a gesture of disgust and for a time was busy shucking out casings and plugging in fresh loads. When her dark gaze returned to his face she said, 'I wasn't in any danger, except from you. My hip hurts worse than it did before.' She spun away. He watched her walk the full distance to the front barn opening and halt to listen briefly before she stepped out front. He lost sight of her as she went along the front of the barn as far as the bunkhouse. He held his breath but there was no gunshot from the house.

He beat dust off with his hat, also walked up to the front of the barn, leaned, saw her moving across the small front porch of the bunkhouse and his breath stopped again. She was striding in plain sight across the yard in the direction of the main house.

He was rigid. She neither increased her gait nor slackened it. Something reflected darkly from the doorway. Evan shot from the hip, a snap-shot. The Winchester in the doorway blossomed briefly orange. Evan fired again. This time the saddle gun rattled noisily across the porch planking.

Lee Bovard had not fired. She reached the lowest step and was poised to take another step when a massive shadow appeared in the doorway, bellowed and charged.

Evan waited two seconds for her to raise the gun in her hand and fire. The large bellowing outlaw hit her full force.

They went down in a writhing tangle as Evan sprinted forward. There was no mistaking that bear-like snarling growl. Sam McDermot had her pinned. He was roaring curses as he raised a gun, which was when Evan hit him head-on. They both rolled clear of Lee Bovard, who did not move.

The retarded McDermot had the strength of a bear. He was wild-eyed and never stopped bellowing. Evan tried to roll clear but the large man clung to him with his left arm as he raised his right fist which was holding the six-gun.

Evan hit McDermot in the chest. For all the effect of the blow he might as well have struck an oak stump.

He twisted as the gun started to descend. There was a loud explosion close by, muzzleblast limned everything for a fraction of a second before McDermot went sideways as though struck by an invisible fist. The descending six-gun fell heavily.

Evan pushed clear and rolled up to his feet.

Behind and to his right someone cocked a gun. The second shot punched McDermot where he was sprawled. Evan twisted half around, saw the gun being aimed for the third shot and said, 'He's dead.'

She fired anyway.

12

Thank You, Ma'am, But No Thanks!

Lee Bovard got up, six-gun hanging at her side. Without a word or a glance she climbed the steps kicked the door wide open and raised her six-gun. She called from the parlour. Evan responded with a wince. Sam McDermot was not just large he was massively heavy; when that kind of a man attacked it was with the fury, weight and power of a boar bear.

The room was a shambles. The man on the floor was as thick and powerful as Sam, but several inches shorter. Evan leaned for a closer look as the woman said, 'Broken neck,' and sank down into an old leather chair.

Evan arose nodding. 'He must have snuck around back to get in.'

She methodically reloaded her

handgun without speaking, but when she arose she said, 'If this is what we came here for, we did it, now let's go home.'

Evan said, 'Tex . . . ?'

'You're the lawman, go find him. I'm going home.'

She left the house in the direction of the barn. He watched from the doorway as she led her animal out of the barn, swung into the saddle and solemnly regarded him as she said, 'They need me at home,' and left the yard riding at a steady walk. He watched until she was out of sight. She had been right about it being over — for her. He ached in places most men didn't even have places.

He was in the middle of the yard when four riders appeared, riding without haste. He got as far as the tie-rack before stopping to lean and wait.

They were weathered, faded, unsmiling men. Where they stopped to look at the leaning man, one said, 'My name's

Morford. We heard shootin', sounded like a damned war. Who are you?'

'Evan Stannard, marshal down at Rock City. You gents friends of the McDermots?'

The man named Morford drew himself up in the saddle. 'Neighbours, Marshal. McDermots had no friendly neighbours.'

'There are two dead, one out on the porch, one in the house and another dead one in the barn.' As Evan finished speaking the four riders gazed in stony silence at him, right up until he turned his back on them to enter the barn, then they dismounted, spoke cryptically among themselves before two headed for the house and the man named Morford and a companion followed Evan into the barn.

Off in the distant east there was a red sliver of dawnlight beneath a fishbelly sky.

Evan got a horse from out back, picked up the first saddle and blanket he saw while one of the strangers fitted a bridle. When the horse was ready Evan pointed toward the shattered door of a stall. 'He's in there,' he said, and led the horse outside before mounting. Only the man named Morford followed Evan. As the lawman was preparing to mount Morford said, 'You done this alone?'

Evan swung across leather. 'No. I had a woman along.'

Morford was standing like a statue when the other man came up. He said, 'There was a woman with him, Jeb. He didn't do this alone.'

Dawn was breaking as Evan picked up the tracks Ordway had made. Fortunately new-daylight made it possible for him to follow the sign of a running horse. Running horses dug in hard with their rear hooves. It helped too that this near the yard the graze had been cropped close.

It was cold, something Evan scarcely noticed. As daylight increased he was able to see a considerable distance. He was the only moving creature until the tracks veered southerly, and he began encountering bands of cattle, mostly they had recently arisen from their beds. Because it was only one rider and he was travelling slow, the cattle watched without moving away.

A dog coyote came up over a lip of land, saw the mounted man and fled, running so fast his guard hairs brushed the ground.

Twice he picked his way with care through prairie dog villages, each such place covered about an acre of land.

Ordway's tracks passed directly through both villages and Evan shook his head. A running horse passing through a rodent village had about as much chance of not breaking a leg as a man had of sprouting wings.

Heat came into the new day, the numbers of cattle he encountered increased as they grazed along. Another time he would have looked for brands, this morning he scarcely more than glanced at the cattle.

Eventually the landscape changed;

trees stood together or as individuals.

With a climbing sun over his shoulder he halted once to water the horse and here, where the tracks met the creek, they had splashed across without hesitation. Evan shook his head. Ordway's horse would end up wind broke if the man didn't start favouring it.

Once, he saw a rider. The man was dusting along a little band of cattle, probably first-calf heifers. If he saw Evan he gave no indication of it.

He stopped on a top-out. Ordway's tracks were heading directly for the wild uplands, not an encouraging state of affairs. A fleeing man, one who knew the wild country, could establish a bushwhack with ease, and if he had been watching for pursuit and had seen a rider dogging him across miles of open country he most certainly would be waiting up ahead.

Heat on the back as much as the steady, rhythmic gait of his horse made staying awake difficult. For yards at a time he did not watch the sign. He told the horse he would cheerfully give a year's wages to lie in the shade of a tree and sleep for a week.

The animal had begun to understand what the man wanted him to do miles back; follow tracks. It ploughed along on slack reins without deviating. Its rider dozed, jerked awake and dozed.

The horse missed a lead. Normally because this jarred riders, the man riding the horse would have sprung awake and alert. Not this time.

The horse walked along head up, little ears pointing its full attention on something about half a mile ahead. When it missed its lead a second time Evan's eyes opened wide.

What had caught and held his mount's attention was another horse, head-hung, ridden down and favouring. Everything was in place except that the saddle was empty. The little danger-bells in the back of Evan's mind were pealing. The closer he got to the riderless animal the more his horse stiffened its gait. When they were less than gun-range apart the head-hung animal slowly lifted its head. It was favouring its right leg, barely allowing the hoof to touch the ground. It gimped a little and stopped when the pain started. While it had been moving Evan made his judgement. Whatever had lamed the horse, a prairie dog hole or an accident arising from exhaustion, the injury was in the shoulder not the ankle.

He drew rein and while the horses eyed each other Evan studied the countryside. There were several bosques of trees and southward not far from the beginning of the rugged foothills of the uplands, there were thick, sprawling patches of chaparral as well as a number of tree-like, red-barked manzanitas.

Evan watched for a reflection, did not see any and was leaning to dismount when the gunshot sounded. If he had remained upright in the saddle the bushwhacker probably would have scored. Because he had his right foot out of the stirrup and was leaning to swing down, the bullet struck a distant bush behind him causing dozens of little coin-sized leaves to fall.

Evan had the horse between himself and the bushwhacker. If the assassin had not been concentrating on Evan he could have shot the lawman's horse; putting his enemy afoot miles from anywhere would have increased his chances of escaping. The obvious reason why he wanted Evan's horse alive kept the lawman close to the animal.

Smokeless powder had its advantages; try as he might he could not locate the area where the gunshot had originated.

Evan leaned across the saddle and called loudly. This was one of those times when a lie was justified. He said, 'There's riders coming, Tex. They'll hang you sure as hell. Stand up an' throw out your guns. I'll take you back to Rock City. You'll get a fair trial.'

The reedy-voiced Texan called back, 'Ain't no riders comin'. I can see for fifty miles. Get away from the horse an' keep both hands in sight. I won't shoot you. Walk out a-ways from the horse.'

Evan continued to lean across the saddle seat. He placed the area of the Texan's shout but he also knew anyone as experienced as the former Three Bells' range boss would have been moving as he had called back.

'You're the only one left,' Evan called and got back a succinct reply. 'Where's the she-devil?'

'Behind you somewhere. Between you'n the uplands.'

'Get away from the damned horse. *Now!*'

Evan continued to lean across the saddle. 'If you get away,' he shouted back, 'you'll never make it out of the country. You know some stockman named Morford?'

'Get away from the horse!'

'Morford and some others met me in the yard back yonder. Whether you can see 'em or not, they'll be along.'

This time the Texan's response was pitched higher and was unmistakably murderous. 'For the last time, you son of a bitch, get away from the horse!'

Evan saw bushes quiver near the place he thought the voice had sounded. He raised his six-gun to the saddle seat and fired three times, once to the left, once to the right and dead centre.

There was no return fire, nor did the underbrush quiver again.

Evan's horse had reacted to having a gun go off across his back the way any horse would have reacted. He gave one tremendous leap forward, lit down and did not stop until he was beside the lame animal.

Evan had lost his cover. He moved, sashaying as he went. There still was no gunfire.

The sun had reached its meridian and was beginning the long, slow slide downward as Evan zigzagged toward the yonder thickets.

His six-gun flashed upwards tracking brief frantic movement when he was less than a hundred feet from the foremost stands of underbrush.

A grey brush rabbit larger than a small dog burst out of the brush running wildly. Evan came within seconds of shooting the rabbit. It changed course every few yards. During its last change it came within ten feet of Evan before veering in a different direction.

Evan exhaled a ragged breath, his legs trembled. For several moments he stood in one place before resuming his stalk.

The mystery Evan never satisfactorily resolved to his personal satisfaction caught and held his attention as he pushed in among the thorny bushes.

Tex Ordway was held off the ground by a particularly thick chaparral bush. He was face up, bent in the middle. His eyes were already drying. The bullet which had killed him had come from below. His right fist was closed, vice-like, around the handle of a sixgun. Possibly a wiry bush had snapped the reloading trap open. Ordway had gone backward over a bush as he fell. The bullet had struck him high in the chest. There were several bullets on the ground. The horses were picking grass a hundred or so yards, the ridden-down animal favouring his right foreleg with every step.

Evan sat in sunlight trying to sort through what he saw. His eventual conclusion was correct but as long as he lived he remained unconvinced despite the evidence.

Ordway had been in the act of reloading. The little hinged reloading chute was open. Somehow or other, perhaps while he'd been in the act of ducking away from the lawman's last three shots, Tex Ordway had pushed into the bushes, where a wiry branch had snugged back the hammer and either Ordway had tightened his grip to pull the six-gun clear of the brush or another limb of underbrush had got caught inside the trigger guard or had possibly snagged the hammer, but whichever had happened, the gun Ordway had been in the act of reloading had fired upwards killing the man with his own weapon.

Nickering horses brought Evan out of his shocked reverie. He shoved Ordway's pistol into his britches, went to his horse, got astride and with the lame horse painfully following struck out in search of the coach road.

They camped atop the spine of the stage road. Evan ate Ordway's store of food from the dead man's saddle-bags.

In the morning, the lame horse had to limp a good mile before it warmed out enough to make the ride back downslope which was prolonged and tedious.

He encountered no one, only once was his attention abruptly caught and held. A 600 pound black boar bear ambled out into the road, sat down and vigorously scratched, indifferent to the scent of a rider.

Evan waited. The bear straightened up, looked a long moment in the direction of the motionless horse and rider, made one of those bear grunts, part whine, part growl, crossed the road and disappeared among the trees.

Evan smiled but his horses did not untuck their tails for a long mile.

As the logged-off lower slope made it possible for the marshal to see bright sunshine reflecting off open country, he scratched a stubby jaw and after the custom of riders talked to his horse. There were several subjects to be mentioned and one subject he did not talk about: Lee Bovard, whose intriguing swift smile and handsome features had half won his heart.

He only mildly entertained critical thoughts. She had proven as tough and willing as any man he'd ever ridden with. She was as good a sign reader as he'd ever known, and she had courage enough for the two of them.

She had also stood behind him in the barn and shot a wounded man who was weak as a kitten, had then walked away without a second glance or a word.

He agreed that she had probably saved his life when the enraged McDermot had knocked him down, straddled him and raised his six-gun to brain him. She had shot McDermot. He owed her for that. She had then stood up and deliberately shot a dead man.

After getting jumped off her horse in the arroyo she had lit into Evan like a she-bear. She was entitled to have a temper; Evan also had one, but Lee Bovard's temper went past anger.

His reverie ended when his horse picked up the gait. It had caught the scent of hay and water. It fought the bit. Evan dismounted and led both animals. It was late in the day, dusk was forming. Those who saw him enter Rock City passed word of his return.

At the livery barn where Mark Wheeler was performing his nightly balancing act on a rickety chair as he turned up the wick of the runway lantern, the liveryman almost fell as he craned around to watch the lawman lead in two saddled animals.

Mike Dougherty and the harness-maker appeared simultaneously as the liveryman was leading the horses away to be cared for, shaking his head in disapproval with every step.

Dougherty waited until Evan was seated then offered a pony of brandy from a hip pocket, while the harness-maker simply stood like stone, staring. Eventually, he softly said, 'Chris'almighty Evan, you look like somethin' a pup'd drag in from a tanyard.'

Evan swallowed twice from Dougherty's bottle, handed it back and smiled. 'How are the prisoners?'

The liveryman was returning from out back and stopped dead in his tracks. The harness-maker cleared his throat before speaking. 'We hanged 'em Evan.'

Stannard stood up nodding his head. 'I'm goin' to bed. Mike, I'd take it kindly if you'd let me take that bottle along.'

The three men stood in dusk-gloom watching the lawman pass his jailhouse and look neither right nor left all the way up to the rooming-house. Frank looked at Mike Dougherty. 'He didn't hear me.'

The saloonman answered brusquely. 'He heard you. Lads, he's wore down to a nubbin' an' I wouldn't bet a plugged cartwheel he don't come out of his room for a week. He looks like hell.'

Dougherty was almost right. Marshal Stannard didn't appear until late the following evening. He went to the jailhouse, visited his empty cages, eased down at the desk and groped for his lower desk drawer. He did not light a lamp until well past supper-time. His old friends from the harness works and the saloon told folks to leave him alone, and for the most part they did. The next morning he was the caféman's first customer. He was gone before the regulars appeared to ask the caféman what he'd said. The caféman was truthful. 'He said steak, spuds and leave the coffee pot on the counter.'

'That's all?'

'That's every damned word.'

The harness-maker entered the jailhouse nodded to Evan, sat in the chair against the east wall and told Evan folks thought he'd been killed. The answer Frank got was curt. 'Some other fellers but not me. You knew Tex Ordway?'

'Yes.'

'Well, he was the last to die. The son of a bitch'd been stealing Three Bells' cattle for years, driving them north an' deliverin' them to some thieves named McDermot. They're dead too. Frank . . . who lynched my prisoners?'

The harness-maker changed position in the chair as he said, 'Leave it be, Evan. It was good riddance.'

'Frank!'

'The whole town, Evan. You want to arrest the whole town?'

Evan leaned back in his chair. 'You know that niece of Jim Bovard's? She went with me.'

The harness-maker's gaze did not

leave the marshal's face. 'I heard she could read sign,' he said. 'She stayed with you the full distance?'

'Right up to the last day. Frank, I never saw a woman who'd shoot like she did.'

The harness-maker left. In late afternoon a neat top buggy tied up in front of the jailhouse. It's solitary passenger entered the jailhouse and threw Evan a warm fleeting smile. Lee Bovard was scrubbed shiny, her split skirt and shirt were immaculate. As she removed her gloves she said, 'You found him, didn't you?'

Evan nodded.

'I told my uncle what he'd done over the years with Three Bells' cattle.'

'How is your uncle?'

'They're all on the mend. He said to tell you he owed you an' he'd repay. I can tell you from knowin' him a long time that he never forgets a right nor a wrong . . . Evan?'

'Yes'm.'

'We were together a long time.'

'Seems longer than it was,' he told her dryly.

She pulled the doeskin gloves through her fingers and did not look at him when next she spoke. 'I guess we got to know each other.'

He nodded about that.

She raised her eyes. 'If you'd be of a mind you could call on me.'

Evan's expression did not change as he arose behind the desk. 'Lee, you can do better.'

She also arose. 'If you're willing I'd be willing.'

He held the door for her, waited until she waved and drove away then leaned in the doorway as he quietly said, 'If it's all the same to you, ma'am, I don't think I'm of a mind.'

THE END

Other titles in the Linford Western Library

THE CROOKED SHERIFF
John Dyson

Black Pete Bowen quit Texas with a burning hatred of men who try to take the law into their own hands. But he discovers that things aren't much different in the silver mountains of Arizona.

THEY'LL HANG BILLY FOR SURE:
Larry & Stretch
Marshall Grover

Billy Reese, the West's most notorious desperado, was to stand trial. From all compass points came the curious and the greedy, the riff-raff of the frontier. Suddenly, a crazed killer was on the loose — but the Texas Trouble-Shooters were there, girding their loins for action.

RIDERS OF RIFLE RANGE
Wade Hamilton

Veterinarian Jeff Jones did not like open warfare — but it was there on Scrub Pine grass. When he diagnosed a sick bull on the Endicott ranch as having the contagious blackleg disease, he got involved in the warfare — whether he liked it or not!

BEAR PAW
Nevada Carter

Austin Dailey traded two cows to a pair of Indians for a bay horse, which subsequently disappeared. Tracks led to a secret hideout of fugitive Indians — and cattle thieves. Indians and stockmen co-operated against the rustlers. But it was Pale Woman who acted as interpreter between her people and the rangemen.

THE WEST WITCH
Lance Howard

Detective Quinton Hilcrest journeys west, seeking the Black Hood Bandits' lost fortune. Within hours of arriving in Hags Bend, he is fighting for his life, ensnared with a beautiful outcast the town claims is a witch! Can he save the young woman from the angry mob?

GUNS OF THE PONY EXPRESS
T. M. Dolan

Rich Zennor joined the Pony Express venture at the start, as second-in-command to tough Denning Hartman. But Zennor had the problems of Hartman believing that they had crossed trails in the past, and the fact that he was strongly attached to Hartman's Indian girl, Conchita.

BLACK JO OF THE PECOS
Jeff Blaine

Nobody knew where Black Josephine Callard came from or whither she returned. Deputy U.S. Marshal Frank Haggard would have to exercise all his cunning and ability to stay alive before he could defeat her highly successful gang and solve the mystery.

RIDE FOR YOUR LIFE
Johnny Mack Bride

They rode west, hoping for a new start. Then they met another broken-down casualty of war, and he had a plan that might deliver them from despair. But the only men who would attempt it would be the truly brave — or the desperate. They were both.

THE NIGHTHAWK
Charles Burnham

While John Baxter sat looking at the ruin that arsonists had made of his log house, a stranger rode into the yard. Baxter and Walt Showalter partnered up and re-built the house. But when it was dynamited, they struck back — and all hell broke loose.

MAVERICK PREACHER
M. Duggan

Clay Purnell was hopeful that his posting to Capra would be peaceable enough. However, on his very first day in town he rode into trouble. Although loath to use his .45, Clay found he had little choice — and his likeness to a notorious bank robber didn't help either!

SIXGUN SHOWDOWN
Art Flynn

After years as a lawman elsewhere, Dan Herrick returned to his old Arizona stamping ground to find that nesters were being driven from their homesteads by ruthless ranchers. Before putting away his gun once and for all, Dan forced a bloody and decisive showdown.

RIDE LIKE THE DEVIL!
Sam Gort

Ben Trunch arrived back on the Big T only to find that land-grabbing was in progress. He confronted Luke Fletcher, saloon-keeper and town boss, with what was happening, and was immediately forced to ride for his life. But he got the chance to put it all right in the end.

SLOW WOLF AND DAN FOX:
Larry & Stretch
Marshall Grover

The deck was stacked against an innocent man. Larry Valentine played detective, and his investigation propelled the Texas Trouble-Shooters into a gun-blazing fight to the finish.

BRANAGAN'S LAW
Alan Irwin

To Angus Flint, the valley was his domain and he didn't want any new settlers. But Texas Ranger Jim Branagan had other ideas. Could he put an end to Flint's tyranny for good?

THE DEVIL RODE A PINTO
Bret Rey

When a settler is cut to ribbons in a frenzied attack, Texas Ranger Sam Buck learns that the killer is Rufus Berry, known as The Devil. Sam stiffens his resolve to kill or capture Berry and break up his gang.

THE DEATH MAN
Lee F. Gregson
The hardest of men went in fear of Ford, the bounty hunter, who had earned the name 'The Death Man'. Yet even Ford was not infallible — when he killed the wrong man, he found that he was being sought himself by the feared Frank Ambler.

LEAD LANGUAGE
Gene Tuttle
After Blaze Colton and Ricky Rawlings have delivered a train load of cows from Arizona to San Francisco, they become involved in a load of trouble and find themselves on the run!

A DOLLAR FROM THE STAGE
Bill Morrison
Young saddle-tramp Len Finch stumbled into a web of murder, lawlessness, intrigue and evil ambition. In the end, he put his life on the line for the folks that he cared about.

BRAND 2: HARDCASE
Neil Hunter

When Ben Wyatt and his gang hold up the bank in Adobe, Wyatt is captured. Judge Rice asks Jason Brand, an ex-U.S. Marshal, to take up the silver star. Wyatt is in the cells, his men close by, and Brand is the only man to get Adobe out of real trouble . . .

THE GUNMAN AND THE ACTRESS
Chap O'Keefe

To be paid a heap of money just for protecting a fancy French actress and her troupe of players didn't seem that difficult — but Joshua Dillard hadn't banked on the charms of the actress, and the fact that someone didn't want him even to reach the town . . .

HE RODE WITH QUANTRILL
Terry Murphy

Following the break-up of Quantrill's Raiders, both Jesse James and Mel Becher head their own gang. A decade later, their paths cross again when, unknowingly, they plan to rob the same bank — leading to a violent confrontation between Becher and James.

THE CLOVERLEAF CATTLE COMPANY
Lauran Paine

Bessie Thomas believed in miracles, and her husband, Jawn Henry, did not. But after finding a murdered settler and his woman, and running down the renegades responsible, Jawn Henry would have time to reflect. He and Bessie had never had children. Miracles evidently did happen.

COOGAN'S QUEST
J. P. Weston
Coogan came down from Wyoming on the trail of a man he had vowed to kill — Red Sheene, known as The Butcher. It was the kidnap of Marian De Quincey that gave Coogan his chance — but he was to need help from an unexpected quarter to avoid losing his own life.

DEATH COMES TO ROCK SPRINGS
Steven Gray
Jarrod Kilkline is in trouble with the army, the law, and a bounty hunter. Fleeing from capture, he rescues Brian Tyler, who has been left for dead by the three Jackson brothers. But when the Jacksons reappear on the scene, will Jarrod side with them or with the law in the final showdown?

GHOST TOWN
J. D. Kincaid

A snowstorm drove a motley collection of individuals to seek shelter in the ghost town of Silver Seam. When violence erupted, Kentuckian gunfighter Jack Stone needed all his deadly skills to secure his and an Indian girl's survival.

INCIDENT AT LAUGHING WATER CREEK
Harry Jay Thorn

All Kate Decker wants is to run her cattle along Laughing Water Creek. But Leland MacShane and Dave Winters want the whole valley to themselves, and they've hired an army of gunhawks to back their play. Then Frank Corcoran rides right into the middle of it . . .

THE BLUE-BELLY SERGEANT
Elliot Conway

After his discharge from the Union army, veteran Sergeant Harvey Kane hoped to settle down to a peaceful life. But when he took sides with a Texas cattle outfit in their fight against redlegs and reb-haters, he found that his killing days were far from over.

BLACK CANYON
Frank Scarman

All those who had robbed the train between Warbeck and Gaspard were now dead, including Jack Chandler, believed to be the only one who had known where the money was hidden. But someone else did know, and now, years later, waited for the chance to lift it . . .

LOWRY'S REVENGE
Ron Watkins

Frank Lowry's chances of avenging the murder of his wife by Sol Wesley are slim indeed. Frank has never fired a Colt revolver in anger, and he is up against the powerful Wesley family . . .

THE BLACK MARSHAL
John Dyson

Six-guns blazing, The Black Marshal rides into the Indian Nations intent upon imposing some law and order after his own family has been killed by desperadoes. Who can he trust? Only Judge Colt can decide.

KILLER'S HARVEST
Vic J. Hanson

A money man and a law deputy were murdered and a girl taken hostage by four badmen who went on the run. But they failed to reckon on veteran gunfighter Jay Lessiter, or on Goldie Santono's bandidos.